AN ABUSE OF JUSTICE

Roger Parkes was born in Chingford in 1933 and educated at Epsom College. After service in the RAF he graduated in Agriculture and then spent several years in journalism, culminating as a foreign correspondent with the *Daily Express*. More recently he has worked as a television scriptwriter, contributing to such popular series as *Crown Court*, *Z-Cars*, *The Expert*, and *The Onedin Line*, also creating and writing two television series for young people, *Them & Us* and *Y-E-S*. His first crime novel, *Riot*, is also available in Collins Crime. He is married with two children and lives in Berkshire.

GW00707804

by the same author

Riot

ROGER PARKES

An Abuse of Justice

FONTANA/Collins

First published in Great Britain by
William Collins Sons & Co. Ltd, 1988
First published in Fontana Paperbacks 1989

Copyright © Roger Parkes 1988

Made and printed in Great Britain by
William Collins Sons & Co. Ltd, Glasgow

PART ONE

Chapter One

There was something odd about the class. Mrs Walton sensed it instantly as she greeted Four C back in from the lunch-break: unnaturally silent and watchful, tension seeping from one child to the other. Yet whereas the majority sensed it intuitively while remaining uncertain of why or what, there were two, seated to one side, who very clearly did know.

'Vicky Bates, are you all right?' It was obvious that she was not: the eight-year-old's face deeply flushed, the eyes red and puffy, her posture hunched and furtive in the desk she shared with Lucy Morton. 'Vicky, what have you been up to?'

Whatever it was had, moreover, robbed the usually loud child of both tongue and cheekiness.

'Lucy?' It was equally obvious that the blushing Lucy Morton knew very well, straggly little wimp. 'At the circus during lunch-break, were you?'

Not hard to guess that much, what with it set out like a honey trap beside the school. Before she could confirm it, however, the teacher saw the tears starting down Vicky's cheeks and decided it was corridor time. She fetched a tissue for the child and led her quickly outside. 'You as well, Lucy. Come along.'

There was something odd, she noticed, about the little girl's movements, the shoulders hunched but also a strange, mincing shift to her walk. It worried the teacher, giving substance to the anxiety which haunted her as remorselessly as it did all those in the Marlbury area with care of primary-school youngsters.

The tears were in full flood by the time Mrs Walton

had the two girls outside. Impulsively she reached out in sympathy, but Vicky swung away, pushing her face into the corner where the corridor turned along towards the main entrance.

'Well, Lucy?' The other girl shook her head, mouth firmly shut, eyes fixed on her mate. 'I'm not asking you again, Lucy Morton. You will tell me – right now – what happened to upset Vicky like this. *Now*, Lucy.'

'Promised not to say, Miss.' It came out as the merest of whispers, the words all but lost in the sobs of her friend. 'Promised.'

'A man? Was it a man?' Lucy's mousy head bobbed once in a single jerk of confirmation. 'Along at the circus, was he?'

Another head jerk. 'He said . . .' The whisper shrank away as Vicky flapped an urgent hand for silence from the corner.

'Come along then to Mr Green. Both of you.'

Briefly, as the teacher took her arm, Vicky clung to the corner before submitting to the firmness of Mrs Walton's grip. The awkwardness of gait was there again as they moved along to the deputy head's office.

Warren Green, hungry as ever for responsibility, had welcomed the school head's departure on yet another course. But he could well have done without this particular call on his initiative.

'One for the nurse,' the teacher murmured, shuffling the two eight-year-olds into the office and nodding discreetly towards Vicky. 'Some man across at the circus.'

'You're sure?'

'Sure enough.'

'But listen . . .'

'Yes, I'm sure!' With which, pulling the door to, she was off along to the school surgery.

'Just you, Vicky?' To his relief, the deputy head detected a subdued nod from Lucy Morton who, awed by this escalation of authority, was herself fast approaching tears. 'You saw the man, too, Lucy?' Nod. 'And what? He told you not to tell anyone or else?' Another nod. 'Was he a stranger? You didn't recognize him?' Headshake, this time in denial. 'And Vicky? Did she seem to know him?'

He caught the final headshake as the school nurse came in ahead of Mrs Walton, her face flushed with concern as she moved to comfort the miserable Vicky.

'Okay for now, Lucy,' he told her, 'just pop along back to class with Mrs Walton. Cheer up. Vicky'll be fine now she's with Nurse.'

If only, he thought ruefully as they left, if only one could so readily erase the wrongs of others.

'He, er, the man touched you, did he, Vicky?' The child, lacking a corner, hunched against the nurse. 'He did things to you? Then warned you not to tell?' It was hard to be sure whether the motion of the tousled mop of auburn hair was due to sobs or nods.

'I checked the register,' the nurse murmured. 'There's no record of her being at risk in the past.'

'Fine. Good.'

So far Warren Green had manifested an outward composure and authority appropriate, he felt, to a school head. Yet insecurity was welling up fast with the hardening of the nightmare suspicions. Briefly, his face stiff with shock and uncertainty, he saw the nurse's outraged expression as she glanced at him over Vicky's head. What next! What else should he say or do before he started to make phone calls and let things go irrevocably beyond the school?

Abruptly the deputy head made the decision, reaching for the telephone, glad to avoid the nurse's eyes but alarmed at the prospect of his first-ever nine-nine-nine call.

'Emergency. Which service do you require?'

'Police.'

Pause for clicks. 'Marlbury Police, who's calling please?'

'Er, this is Warren Green, Box Common Primary School. I have a child here who, er, has apparently been, er, physically molested by a stranger.'

'Box Common. Right, sir, we'll have a WPC round to you directly. Have either of the parents been notified?'

'I'll get on to that straight away.' He hung up, reaching for the address register and trying to recall what, if anything, he knew of the Bates family. At best, all he could manage was a vague image of a sandy-haired woman with a fag in her mouth.

'Vicky, we'll need to find your mum.'

This time there was no mistaking the rejection in the child's headshake. He found and dialled their home number, listened in vain to the ringing tone, wondered what the heck next, and then nodded as he realized the nurse was signalling for his attention.

'A social worker I know,' she murmured. 'Janet Heanley. She specializes in this sort of thing.'

But what sort of thing? Already assumptions and alarm bells, police and parents; and all on a show of distress and a few startled whispers.

He gave up on the Bates home, rang off and beckoned for Nurse to ease the girl closer to the desk. 'Vicky love, we have to find your mum or dad. Any ideas?' This brought snuffles and a mutter from behind the tissue. 'Say again?'

'Something about her mum working as a cleaner.'

'Do you know where?' Headshake. 'Nor your dad?' Headshake. 'Janet Heanley?' he asked, searching for the social services number.

'That's right. Experienced in these cases.'

Some qualification: authority on the handiwork of monsters!

The social services number was engaged. He redialled just in case, then rang off just as the policewoman arrived. Although she was dressed in uniform, she had it largely concealed beneath a bright tweed coat. A warm, homely young woman.

'WPC Hobbs, sir. I had a message from the station. Is this the little lady in question?'

The deputy head introduced Vicky, then supplied her address and the names of her parents. 'Not too clear,' he explained, 'but it seems Vicky slipped off to the circus with her mate during lunch-break and some man, er . . .'

'You've tried to contact the parents?'

'Both at work.'

'I'll phone the police surgeon, all right?'

'Well, of course, if you think it's necessary.'

'Can't proceed, sir, without a physical.'

'We were trying to contact Miss Heanley,' the nurse put in with sudden firmness.

'The social worker? Yes, good. Ask her to liaise at the surgery, then.'

Connected to the surgery, the policewoman confirmed that Dr Shanks was on call, then arranged for a priority examination.

'Okay, Vicky? All set to go?' It was clear that, on the contrary, Vicky was not set to go anywhere. Whatever fate she had suffered in the lunch-break, the prospect of this next ordeal was evidently worse. 'Fancy a ride in a police car, don't you? Nurse'll be along as well if that'll help.'

It did help, the prospect of elevated status further sweetening the dreaded pill of the unknown. None the less, it was only with renewed sobs that the child allowed herself to be led outside. Shock and pain notwithstanding, it was a major trauma to be the focus of all this attention, fuss and bustle. As Mrs Walton observed later to the deputy head: 'Vicky's a scamp and a pain in class, but she lacks the imagination to come on with all that sobbing and upset merely as a deception.'

'Nurse will help you with your clothes, Vicky. Have to undress, you see, for the examination. All right?'

Dr Shanks was not insensitive, far from it. But experience over many years, both as a police surgeon and a GP, had prompted a certain briskness at this stage of the proceedings. Child victims were often deeply shocked, often in pain, invariably bewildered and as scared by the subsequent chain of events as by the incident itself. Moreover, this physical examination, essentially clinical and comprehensive, could seem as much of an assault as the incident itself. Yet there was no way it could be either avoided, delayed or modified. So that an initial briskness of manner could help to counter the victim's hysteria, overt or repressed, and make the doctor's later switch to sympathy the more effective.

He noticed with relief that the underpants, although grubby, showed no sign of blood, indicating restraint on the part of the molester – if indeed there had been molestation at all. However, it was apparent, even before they reached the examination-couch stage, that there was genital damage.

'You've seen doctors' instruments before, Vicky? The stethoscope, see, to listen to your chest.' He did so, heart and lungs, front and back, then showed her the ophthalmoscope before examining her eyes and ears.

'Now the spatula. Mouth open, tongue out.' No throat bruising apparent, thank God. 'Fine – that's your ears, throat, eyes and chest all clear and in the pink. Now let's have a look at your botty. Is that what you call it? My young daughter, Philippa, calls it her down below. Just lie back on the couch then, the way nurse shows you. That's it. Philippa went to Thorpe Park for her birthday treat the other day. Have you been there, Vicky?'

He caught the nurse's eye, nodding as she launched chattily in about how Vicky's whole class had been on an excursion there last summer; how special the water features were, how several of the boys had managed to get themselves soaked, and so on – the diversion working gradually to ameliorate the sobs while the doctor probed and peered methodically, then collected swabs and samples, firstly vaginal and then, with the child rotated, also anal. The latter, although apparently superfluous to judge from the puffy, inflamed state of the urinary end of things, were necessary for the court. Dr Shanks had learned the hard way, through persistent courtroom grillings, the morbid extent of clinical detail with which lawyers sought to impress juries.

Eventually, thanks to the doctor's gentleness and experience, the nurse's attentions and Thorpe Park's seemingly inexhaustible varieties, the examination was over, the sobs along with it.

Distress resumed briefly when Vicky was refused her clothes and instead wrapped in an over-large gown until replacement clothing could be acquired.

'For tests,' the police surgeon explained to her, showing them to her in a plastic bag. 'The detectives, you know, will need to look for clues.'

'In my knickers?' It was Vicky's first coherent remark and signalled a shift from shock and bewilderment back towards the brash Vicky so familiar to Mrs Walton and her Four C class-mates.

Janet Heanley, despite a faultless twenty-two years as a social worker, had shunned promotion. One reason was the changes she'd seen over those twenty-two years, changes in both social and moral attitudes, and also in the nature of her job. Not only was Janet currently carrying double the number of clients from those relaxed earlier years but now she also had the constant worry of *account-ability*. Back in the sixties and early seventies, Janet and her colleagues were locally 'respected' – trusted and mostly welcomed – and were yet to suffer the angry glare of public exposure provoked by the deaths of Tyra Henry, Jasmin Beckford, Heida Koseda, Marie Payne, Kimberly . . . and so on and on.

Besides humiliating Janet and eroding her status with clients, this had also undermined her confidence. Hence, at a time when experience should have enhanced her authority, she instead faced a mounting crisis, assailed not only with a barrage of criticism but also with self-doubts and anxieties which the flow of in-house policy memos and procedural revisions did nothing to allay.

The Permissive Age, so the media sociologists and politicians agreed, was responsible for the decline in school discipline and moral attitudes, for the upsurge in divorce, in illegitimacy and abortion, and for the general erosion of family values. Hence the policy shift away from the parents and on to something called 'the best interests of the child'.

Along with the bad press and the swing to public contempt had also come more frequent abuse and even the threat of violence. Janet herself, small, motherly and warm in appearance for all her spinsterhood, had only been attacked twice, both times by distraught women. But the verbal abuse, ranging from insults to threatened disablement and rape, lingering as it did for days and weeks in her imagination, exacted an increasing toll. Unlike many of her younger colleagues, Janet's vocation for the work was Christian rather than political. Had it been otherwise, she would likely long ago have packed it in.

'Mrs Bates, I'm sorry but I don't know any details. I simply got a message that Vicky's at the surgery for a check-up and would I try to find you.'

'Old busybody Flynn next door – I suppose she said where to find me.' To Janet's irritation, the woman lit up a cigarette. 'Tell her why, did you?'

'Credit me with some tact, Mrs Bates.'

She drove into the surgery forecourt, parked in the staff-reserved bay and escaped the smoke-filled car with relief. So far, about the only endearing thing she'd been able to establish about Mrs Bates was that she and her family had apparently had no previous contact with the social services.

Policewoman Hobbs confirmed this as she met them near the Casualty entrance, passing Janet a note from the medical social worker that Vicky was not on the At Risk register, nor was the family noted on any probation or social services records.

'So come on, then,' the mother asked as the WPC led them along to wait outside Dr Shanks's consulting-room, 'what's Vicky been up to?'

'Her class teacher noticed she was upset and in a state.'

'They been picking on her again?'

'I'm afraid this is more serious, Mrs Bates. There's a man involved. Suspected sexual assault.'

The woman drew breath sharply as she sagged down on to a seat, hands fumbling compulsively for another smoke, the dome of her tight, sandy curls shaking in sharp and emphatic denial.

'No – wrong – she's lying. He'd never touch her. Never!'

Briefly, police officer and social worker exchanged discreet glances.

'Who, Mrs Bates? Vicky's still too shocked to say much.'

'Oh.' She busied herself with the cigarette packet, only to pull a face as Janet pointed to the No Smoking sign. 'Well then, how'd you know it's, like, what you just said?'

'She and her mate Lucy slipped out of the playground during lunch-break and nipped along to the circus.'

'Circus?' Incredibly there was something of relief in the rapid blinking of the mother's eyes. 'You saying it was some bloke down the circus?'

'That's how it looks at this stage.'

'Some stranger?'

'Apparently.'

'Well then.' She gestured, staring from one to the other as indignation asserted itself. 'I mean, what was the school people playing at? Supposed to be supervised, aren't they? Watched over!'

They turned as Dr Shanks opened the door, the mother standing up as he beckoned them into the consulting-room.

'Hello, Mum. Sorry, Mum.'

Vicky, far from running to the woman, hung back, lost and pathetic in the baggy hospital gown. It was the school nurse who went to hug an arm round and move the child across. 'She's been very brave, Mrs Bates. Whole examination and not a word of complaint.'

The mother nodded, bemused and uncertain. 'Where's your clothes, then?'

'Needed for forensic examination,' the doctor explained, fetching the labelled plastic bag which he handed to the WPC before resuming to the mother. 'You'll get them back in due course. Happily there's no need for young Vicky to stay in for observation in the hospital. Just be sure and bring her along here for a check-up tomorrow evening, Mrs Bates, all right?' He turned to the social worker. 'She's just had a wash and clean-up with nurse, so she's all set for the investigative interview.'

The doctor moved across to crouch down and tousle the little girl's hair. 'You can pick up some clothes from your home, Vicky, on the way to Eckersley House.'

'Where's that, then?' the mother asked suspiciously.

'Local authority children's home, Mrs Bates. They've installed special interview facilities there.' Then, in inducement to the child: 'Video cameras and so on. Okay?'

Janet Heanley hung back for a word with the police surgeon as the others filed out to the corridor. She knew better than to expect much in the way of details at this stage. The fact that Dr Shanks had mentioned an investigative interview had been as much confirmation of sexual assault as they could expect. Yet she needed to clarify one aspect.

'Penetration?'

'Digital only.' He nodded.

'Snow, then?'

'Looks like.'

Chapter Two

The interview suite at Eckersley House was new. Achieved by joint funding, it symbolized the new spirit of interdisciplinary collaboration fostered by the Cleveland inquiry: social services premises with police lay-out and equipment. Yet another policy shift for Janet Heanley to adjust to. However, with the attitude and specialized training of the two WPCs on the indecency unit inclining them more and more towards welfare, there was already a blurring of roles. With those two constables as quasi social workers, Janet wondered ruefully, how much was she herself nudging towards quasi cop! Certainly the cumulative emotions of child-abuse work had brought her round to a far more punitive attitude. After all, if the 'best interests of the child' were now paramount, what else but to err towards the victim, albeit of an offence which so often was 'cyclical', learned and repeated generation to generation.

The self-contained interview suite had its own entrance from a side street adjacent to the much-converted old Victorian town house. The interview room itself was small and cosy, with a deep-pile carpet, matching easy chairs, beanbag and a TV set. The only exceptional feature was the large two-way mirror occupying much of one wall. It was behind this mirror that the observation room was situated while, adjoining that, was a small, windowless cubicle with monitor screen and camera controls for the video operator.

'If you'll sit in here, Mrs Bates, you'll be able to watch through the glass. Also there's a microphone so you can hear. I gather there's no chance of contacting your husband to get here.'

'Why can't I be in the room with her?'

WPC Valerie Hobbs smiled reassuringly. 'Procedure, Mrs Bates.'

This wasn't strictly true. Had the mother shown a more sympathetic response, she might have been invited in. As it was, her attitude at the hospital had emphatically disqualified her. Regardless of how innocent Vicky was, the team knew to expect a keen sense of guilt in the child – a sense bound to be aggravated by any show of maternal reproach. Remarks like *she's lying* clearly wouldn't do.

'WPC Crane will be in this adjoining room on the video controls. Anything you may want to say about the conduct of the interview, just pop in and tell her. But do bear in mind, what with the ordeal Vicky's been through, the quicker we can get all this side of it over and done with, preferably without interruptions, the better for her, okay?' Then, pre-empting further objections: 'Miss Crane's brewing up some tea, if you'd like a cuppa.'

The tea, along with biscuits and a can of Coke for Vicky, was all part of the informality calculated to help relax the victim and get her talking.

'Your mum's going to wait in that room there while we have a chat about what happened to you.'

The social worker turned to show the child the magic camera in the corner. 'This is the video camera. And that's you, look, on the TV screen.'

Pause for wonderment and exploration, Jacquie Crane zooming and panning in the control room while Vicky bobbed around the room, enthralled to watch her instant mobility on screen.

'Now, Vicky,' the policewoman intervened, once the novelty was beginning to wear off, 'time to get started. Come over here beside me for the identification.'

She positioned Vicky in front of the large wall clock,

19

nodded for the operator to start taping, stated the date and time, the identity of the child, Janet Heanley and herself. Then she moved the little girl across to sit on the bean-bag while she laid a pile of photographs on a low table in such a way that each could be visible to the camera as presented.

'Okay, Vicky, I know the man said not to tell anyone or else. But the thing is, if we can catch him and get him safely down the nick, then we can keep him away from you. Okay, let's see if you can pick him out among any of these pictures.'

Valerie Hobbs had chosen the pictures with care, selecting a wide variety, including some circus people, clowns and so on, to run through first before showing the child their prime suspect. Vicky, still giggly from the video thought the photos a hoot – not just the circus folk but the tall men, short men, bearded men, black men, the vicar, ice-cream seller – only to freeze, the grin draining from her face, her head swinging involuntarily away in rejection as the twelfth photo was presented.

'What's wrong, Vicky? Look at the picture.'

'No.'

'It's him, is it?'

'Not saying.'

'Take another look so you're absolutely sure. Go on.'

Briefly, fear clouding once again across the freckled features, she turned her head for a second fleeting glimpse before sliding off the bean-bag to pull a frenzied succession of faces for reflection on the video screen. For a moment, to ensure accuracy of the formal record, the police constable held the relevant photograph up again before the camera; so that Vicky, seeing it fill the screen, swung away to fling herself back on to the bean-bag, in the process knocking over the remains of her Coke on to the carpet.

Already, in the video control room, Jacquie Crane was

on the line to the police station and being connected through to the CID room.

'DI Roberts speaking.'

'WPC Crane here, sir. She just IDed Snow, no question.'

'Thanks, Jacquie. We'll pull him in.'

Detective-Inspector Taff Roberts disliked having to run the indecency unit. No denying it was a crucial aspect of police work. But compared with, say, serious crime or even fraud, it was a real penance. The Siberia of appointments. But there it was: the penance had to be served, the *quid pro quo* paid off. Having taken a promotion transfer from the Met to the Thames Valley, there was no way he could just arrive and say 'Sorry, Chief, but no . . . No sex, please. I'm Welsh.'

Moreover, Taff had quit the Met under somewhat of a cloud. Whereas it was an unofficial cloud, with nothing specific written up into his service record, junior inspectors don't cross deputy assistant commissioners with impunity, least of all when the DAC in question is obeying orders from the top which are political and should never have been given.

The problem with indecency was the emotion involved. It was one thing for sentimental birds like Jacquie Crane and Val Hobbs to get all intense and dedicated about the work. But, as Taff Roberts had learned from his old chiefie and mentor at the Yard, the one who's running things must stay objective. Start caring, start getting involved in other than a detached, analytical way, and you risked tripping over prejudices and falling foul of hunches – both death to a career detective's clear-up rate.

Leonard Arthur Snow was a large part of Taff's indecency-unit problem. With most of the villains he had encountered over the years, Taff could at least understand their criminality if not condone it: they were lazy, greedy, bored, opportunistic, impulsive, led into it, brought up to it, whatever; the full range of human frailty. But the sex freaks, particularly the child-sex offenders like Snow, were something else altogether. Worse, Snow was as obsessively sly and cunning as he was hooked on his offence. In the ten years since his first indecency conviction, the man had been arrested more than a dozen times, been charged on ten and prosecuted on six; he had faced four Crown Court jury trials, been acquitted on each; and from all this he had drawn only one other conviction, which had anyway been haggled down to mere common assault. Taff Roberts's predecessor, DI Hargreaves, had been driven to resignation over the man; and, after a couple of years in the indecency seat, Taff knew all too well why.

'Is your husband in, Mrs Snow?'

'Go away! Can't you ever give the poor man a bit of peace!'

She was a small, mousy-haired young woman, her snubbed nose, chubby cheeks and short upper lip lending her face an infantile quality in keeping with the whining tone of her voice. Whether she always whined like this, Taff wasn't to know since he had yet to hear other than complaints and abuse from her.

The retort was on Taff's tongue that only when her husband allowed Marlbury's little girls a bit of peace could he expect any himself. Instead, clearing his throat, he murmured an apology before asking again if the man was at home.

'Wasn't the last time enough for you?' she shrilled. 'Unanimous verdict. Same as the time before. And the time before that. What's wrong with you people? Can't you admit when you're wrong? Learn to take no for an answer? You, mister – you want to try it – see how it feels to be hounded and persecuted!'

'Out the back, is he, Mrs Snow? Out at his collection?'

The woman stood her ground, despair lending courage to her normally cowed nature. But this time the DI was spared further aggro, the husband thrusting her aside, jacket already half on in readiness to leave.

'Give over, Sharon love. Nothing you can say'll get through. Nothing. Just blinkered, aren't they. Just tunnel vision, that's what.'

With which, giving the detective barely more than a glance, he hurried off, light-footed and stoat-like, down the path.

The family of ten physically-explicit dolls lived in a cupboard in a corner of the interview room. Janet Heanley selected only the two appropriate to Vicky's incident for production, however; in this instance the blonde female child doll and the slender adult male doll. Both were normal doll size, differing from shop dolls only in that they had genitals. Both were initially fully clothed so that the re-enactment of the event could be talked through in sequence.

The introduction of the dolls was made with no suggestion of games or fun. After all, what had happened to the child that lunch-break was no game. Moreover, there was the element of catharsis to consider. Whereas a specific explanation of the incident, recorded on video, was the primary objective, the release of fears and emotions would be a crucial bonus for Vicky if skilfully induced . . . yet another reason for excluding less sympathetic or over-protective mothers.

'He came up and talked to you and Lucy while you were looking at the horses?' Janet summarized. 'Then he gave you both some sweeties?'

The child's nod was accompanied by a guilty peep towards the hidden observation room where she knew her mother was watching. *Never take nothing from no stranger, Victoria.*

'Then he promised you more if you went up to where he had his place up in the bushes, that it?' Nod. 'He said he had them hidden up there?' Nod. 'And for Lucy to stay watching the horses while you and him went and fetched them?' Nod.

From past experience, both women knew that this summary, although leading out the child's account, was a necessary prelude to her full and coherent statement. More, they well knew from Snow's prior assaults, the likely stages of his inducements and 'courting'.

'Here, them dolls – they're *disgusting.*'

Jacquie Crane glanced round as Mrs Bates moved indignantly to the doorway of the control room. 'They have to be explicit, madam. Not meant for the nursery.' Then, over-riding the mother's renewed protest, she added: 'What the man did to her, Mrs Bates – that was disgusting, too. If you can think of a better way for Vicky to explain what he did to her, okay. But our experience is that those dolls are the most practical model for description.'

'But that one – the one with the – the . . .'

'A male doll isn't much use for this sort of thing, madam, unless it's got a penis.'

'Disgusting.'

'But necessary – after what he did to the poor kid.'

'Did? What do you mean?'

'Mrs Bates, we don't know exactly – not until Constable Hobbs and the social worker have had a chance to talk it through with her using those disgusting dolls in there.'

Denis Lisle left his Volvo in the car park beneath the law courts reserved for magistrates and court officials, then hurried upstairs and round the fountain towards the adjoining police station. He knew the routine all too well, having acted as Snow's defence solicitor on all his many prior arrests . . . knew, for instance, to expect a cooler than usual reception from the desk sergeant, knew also that the Welsh DI would have chosen interview-room C for the interrogation. He knew, too, pretty well what to expect of his client, including the story he was likely to put up in explanation. It was all consistently depressing, about the only consolation being the fee at the end of it all.

It was not, in point of fact, the fattest of fees, being paid, as it would be, out of legal-aid funds. Indeed, his partners in Reedham & Stott could be tiresomely patronizing about Denis Lisle's criminal defence efforts, those on property conveyancing and company law and even divorce all contributing more richly than the legal-aid side. Yet it was routinely agreed at successive partners' meetings that a certain amount of legal-aid work, along with the Duty Solicitor chore which went with it, were good for the firm's image and, therefore, for old Denny to keep at it . . . which for all his grunts and grumbles, he continued to do, silently preferring the crime work, indeed, to what in his view was their chore work, more profitable though it might be. They were welcome to the squabbles of divorce, the dreariness of property searches or the fastidiousness of contract drafting. Whereas the majority of his court clients might be life's losers – habitual drunks, semi-literate tearaways and inadequates – they were none the less *people*, mostly in genuine need of his help and expertise, rather than mere documents or fiscal manipulations. Denis Lisle may be the poor relation within the firm; yet, by his own secret valuation, he was far and away the richest . . . until, that is, it came to defending Leonard Arthur Snow.

Lisle shared a sour joke with Marlbury Justices' clerk

that each of Snow's arrests had added a year to his life. When you've turned fifty, as he had, it was no joke at all.

Neither the issue of Snow's guilt or innocence nor of Lisle's pre-trial advice to him was of much relevance. Whereas Snow always exercised his right to legal representation, he reckoned he knew it all far better than any lawyer. Although this might have proved intolerable to most, Denis Lisle was of sufficiently subdued, seemingly negative, character to go along with Snow's dictates. Moreover, it enabled him to evade the lurking question of the man's actual guilt or innocence. Like DI Roberts, detachment was essential if Lisle was to do his job properly; so that any such personal judgement was best avoided.

From the professional angle, it helped the solicitor that Snow's defence varied so little from case to case. As so often before, he now sat silently in a corner of the interrogation room, notepad in hand, listening to his client's cold, precise admission that, yes, he had been along at the circus ground that lunch-time watching the equestrian troupe exercising and then grooming their mounts; yes, he had been drawn into conversation with a couple of kiddies in school clothes; asked about the horses, he had explained what he could about them and the circus in general. As a father himself of a toddler, he well knew the importance of patient communication with kiddies. Yes, as it happened, he had bought them both an ice-cream after which they had chased around the park. And yes, so far as he could recall, the ginger-haired one had slipped while walking along the top of a fence, falling astride it and hurting herself down below – well, hurting her bottom then – during the excitement of ragging around. But, no, he most certainly had not touched the child at all, since it would be monstrous to take advantage of a lively youngster like that. As for any injury, that must have been entirely the fall. But, of course, it was plain typical of the witch-hunt mentality of teachers, especially since all this hysteria triggered by Child Line and Cleveland and the like – typical they should go jumping to the wrong conclusions and starting up yet another scare story . . .

The solicitor sat to one side, his pen busy, yet his eyes, like those of the DI and the young WPC assistant, drawn to the suspect Snow . . . who, seemingly with an actor's ability to assimilate his role and believe in his lines, recited his explanation with total conviction, his jaw working methodically on his chewing-gum, his narrowed eyes intense and penetrating, showing little emotion other than an injured innocence.

The solicitor was riveted by the performance, as always, enthralled and chilled by it. And because, unlike the Crown Court juries, he had heard it all so often before, so open and candid and disarmingly simple – because of those dozen or so previous recitations, he was nauseated by it. More, he was grossly ashamed to be present as the callous devil's defender.

Chapter Three

'Isn't Carry ready yet? I've got the car out.'

'Just doing her teeth.'

'Whistle her up, then.'

'No. Clean teeth are more important than . . .'

Jenny Harris thought better of saying 'than his office' and substituted 'than traffic jams'. Jeremy's work was an increasingly touchy topic between them, not least the burgeoning piles of case briefs he brought home each evening.

Jeremy Harris was a criminal lawyer of substantial promise. To have made Branch Crown Prosecutor of the area's Crown Prosecution Service while still under forty was testimony to that. It had helped, no doubt, to have a circuit judge as a father. Yet the care and caution, discretion and correctness, of his professional conduct had ensured success in a world where reliability, even if ponderous, always outweighs the speedy. The law's delays (and profits) are enshrined in tradition; even the whizzkid clients, after all, seldom expect rapid law.

'Mummy said we could all go to Norfolk for John-William's leave weekend.'

'Oh, did she?' Harris changed gear, slowing the car as they reached the tailback on the motorway spur. Every morning it seemed to reach that little bit further back. 'When was this decided?'

'Granny rang yesterday.' Caroline turned to fix him with those dark eyes of hers which, even at ten years old, she already knew how to use. 'Please, Dad-Pa.'

It would have been nice to have had Jenny sound him out on it first – for her to establish, for instance, whether or not he could possibly manage a long weekend away at a time of year when the courts were at peak load. Lately he had begun to suspect his wife of deliberately setting Caroline up to initiate such propositions, knowing he would find it harder to refuse daughter than mother.

'We'll have to see.'

The motorway traffic was moving with average sluggishness, which meant that, subject to unforeseen roadworks, he would drop Carry off at school in time for her assembly and only be fifteen minutes later than he preferred at the office. So long as there were no pre-trial panics among his team of CPS prosecutors, that would be ample. But with the number now up to fifteen, some of them elderly, half of them women, one of them Australian, the chances of no crisis were, to say the least, improbable.

'Not your silly old work again, Dad-Pa.'

'Huh?'

'Norfolk – the granny weekend.'

'Ah.' No doubt another bit of unsubtle lobbying by Jenny. 'I suppose I could take some of it with me.' Then, seeing her pretty face pucker into a grimace: 'Do you actually know what I do – all this "silly old work"?'

'Of course!'

'What?'

'You make laws – send people to prison and – and things.'

'Hah.' The status version, doubtless contrived by Mum to try and impress schoolmates whose fathers all seemed to be in much higher prestige occupations like airline pilots, travel agents, media people and restaurant owners.

In the event, the several case crises were topped, as Harris had known they would be, by that thorniest of CPS issues: careless versus reckless on a fatal traffic accident.

'Megan, I assigned it to you simply because I know

you'll make the right decision on the basis of the evidence and without reference to me.'

'Thanks! All those grieving relatives at the back of the court wanting vengeance! You're a real chum, Jemmy Harris. Power's gone to your head, do you know that. Megalomania. A *real* leader would have gone to court and presented it himself.' Then, pointing at him over her stack of court files, she added with malicious glee: 'Anyway, just to ruin your day as well, the Indecency copper's out there waiting to see you.'

'Not Snow again!'

His response, for a professional of essential unflappability, was unusually sharp and personal, affecting both his tone and his tolerance as he turned to deal with elderly Mrs Palmer's list of quibbles, starting with shoplifting against a 78-year-old widow, rambling on through disorderly behaviour, and ending with the butcher's latest dangerous dog.

It was half an hour before he had soothed, reassured, jollied-up and otherwise coped with all the worries of his family of lawyers – as diverse and perverse in nature as any large family; yet mostly the misfit poor relations by comparison with the fat-cat lawyers in commerce or civil – and went through to begin phase two of his morning.

'Detective-Inspector Roberts has been waiting more than an hour, Mr Harris.'

'Profuse apologies, Inspector,' Harris called, ushering him across to the door of his office. 'Might help if your colleagues in Traffic could get us all moving faster in the mornings.' Not that Carry's teeth-cleaning was going to get any earlier. 'Snow been up to his tricks again? Same as usual?'

'Only that this one's a good deal sooner than usual – not a couple of months since his last effort.'

'His last *reported* effort. We don't know how many he's got away with besides.' How many wee girls with big eyes he had preyed on to gratify his warped lust and then terrorized into staying mute about it. 'Otherwise, the same? Chat up, feed up, fit up, shut up?'

Jeremy Harris was not generally given to such coarseness or to trivializing serious crimes with flippancy; yet there was something about these Snow efforts – their persistence, perhaps, along with the man's arrogant confidence of immunity – which prompted ridicule as a counter to outrage and frustration.

He listened as the detective detailed the circumstances: the circus, the class teacher's initiative, the physical by Dr Shanks, then the investigative interview with its positive identification. Taff Roberts then went on to summarize the initial interview with Snow: the familiar admission of meeting the children but his denials of other than the most innocent of play-romping which had led to the auburn-haired one's fall and localized injury.

'Virtually word for word on the last, Inspector.'

'You'd think he'd vary it a bit.'

'Why should he? He's worked it on numerous juries and they've all swallowed it, so why vary what's proved effective? One thing I'm sure we've both learned about Leonard Snow is not to underestimate him.'

It was said evenly, with no hint of reproach. Yet he could sense from the policeman's rather bullish tone that he was in a mood to have a go on this one. Less pushy than his predecessor, DI Hargreaves, who had let Snow drive him into a breakdown. But none the less, DI Roberts had that same tendency to over-react – to arrest on slender suss, to hammer in interrogation and then press for exaggerated charges – common to coppers when dealing with child sex offences.

'Did the Chief mention it at this morning's press briefing?'

'I imagine he would have done, yes, sir. The Chief's no more fond of Snow than the rest of us.'

And all part, Harris thought to himself, of the same impulse to escalate the CPS – me, in fact – into repeating the same galling process as last time, remanding the menace in custody on indecency charges based on the diciest balance of proof.

'Anything, sir, to keep him off the streets,' the detective added, evidently anticipating the legal objections. Yet it was a desire with which there could be no argument: so long as Snow was indeed guilty, there could be no question but that he was best inside. If the flaw lay with the system of justice – with the principles of law and the technicalities which flowed from it – then it lay with those who operated that flawed system to do what little they could to redress the balance. Provided that Snow was indeed guilty.

'Indecent assault, then?' It was the least they could go for if bail was to be realistically resisted.

'That's how it looks, sir, but we've a few hours still before we're obliged to charge the beggar. We'll hang on in case my team come up with anything this morning.'

'Copper's optimism.'

'Maybe, sir. But you never know. Arrogant bastards like Snow could so often get that bit too cocksure and make a stupid slip.'

Woman Police Constable Hobbs tried to concentrate on the search and ignore the droopy woman watching them from the doorway of Snow's lock-up garage. Sharon Snow had put on her usual defiance when they had arrived with the search warrant, whining on about persecution and vendettas. But now, typically enough, she hung around bleating less in aggression so much as for sympathy while they searched the place, repeating over and over how these recurring police intrusions made any sort of normal domestic existence impossible, the neighbours forever yakking and scorning, shopkeepers cheeking her, even her poor mother at the other side of the estate getting abuse. And what when little Susy got to school age – what then? The poor wee soul would be due to face the same sort of victimization and hatred for sure.

Valerie Hobbs listened and, despite her efforts, found herself yielding to a grudging sympathy. Yet it was tempered by an irreconcilable contradiction, it being beyond her imagination to see how any woman could possibly live with such a creature and remain in ignorance of his perversity. Doubtless Snow denied all to her and wound her up with all these claims of persecution. Yet the very intimacy implicit in the state of marriage seemed to Valerie to make it impossible to sustain such a gross deception. So, accepting that Sharon Snow did know, then she must be prepared, perhaps for the sake of their toddler Susan, both to condone it and, more, to testify at his successive trials to his paternal fondness, reliability and gentleness with kiddies.

'If it's as bad as you say with the neighbours, Mrs Snow, why don't you move away? Go some place where people don't know about him?'

'He says that's no answer,' she sniffed. 'He says that'd be like, you know, giving in to you lot. Besides, he says you'd just tip off the local force to chase him up same as here the moment there was any trouble – accusations and that.'

The WPC was about to take issue with the woman when Jacquie Crane gave an excited cough from the far corner of the garage. Snow used the place not to keep a car in but as a workshop-cum-storeroom for his hobby. As a member of a Civil War re-enactment group, Ensign Snow had fashioned over the years a variety of Royalist uniforms, imitation weapons and props for the staging of battles and skirmishes around the country. For authentication, he had also built up a small library of reference books. WPC Crane's find was concealed in an expensive book of military regalia through the centuries: hidden beneath its protective plastic covering was a small envelope stuffed with photographs of children. They were not the ultra-hard porn of the type circulating throughout the pædophilic subculture, but they were unquestionably suggestive. Originating from Sweden, they featured girls of between six and ten years old, mostly thinly clad or naked and in pseudo Art poses.

'Did you know about these, Mrs Snow?'

It was obvious she did not; moreover, that their discovery was a shock to her. It was several seconds of stunned silence before she hit on an explanation with which she could live and continue to avoid the truth.

'You planted them! You slipped them in there when you thought I wasn't looking. Typical! Never let up, you people!'

'Path lab here.'

'Dr Shanks speaking. Anything on those Victoria Bates swabs?'

'Hang on, please, Doctor, while I go and check.'

The police surgeon, of all those involved in the investigation, was the most cautious. Indeed, he took quiet satisfaction in the fact, well aware of the emotional steam generated in the press by such cases and hence of the threat they posed to expert consultants such as himself. Nor was it solely the spectre of the Cleveland inquiry where medical gurus had publicly contradicted the findings of other medical gurus while the packs of lawyers and MPs had bayed in lament of parental rights and family unity. Of course that legacy was there at the back of Dr Shanks's mind. Yet Cleveland had merely reinforced that caution and reluctance which had been there before, born of prior humiliations in the witness-box.

Can you really be so positive, Doctor? Can you assure the jury that these injuries were inflicted other than by

34

an accident or else by what is sometimes termed Child's Play, the youngster exploring her own genitalia or else doing so with the assistance of a young friend? . . . As a police surgeon, sir, you must be familiar with the pressures on police and other authorities to protect young children from such abuse – pressures seldom far from the hysteria of the witch hunt . . . Can you be absolutely sure, Doctor, that in presenting this jury with the benefit of your opinion, you are not yourself yielding to those same pressures . . . ?

A couple of such assaults on his veracity had been enough for Robin Shanks. The phrase Child's Play had lodged as firmly in his mind as in his subsequent forensic reports, enhanced as it was by dim, pre-pubescent recollections of precisely that: child's play with the neighbour's daughter behind the dense summer growth of raspberry canes at the end of her garden. Nothing exceptional in it, for sure; purely exploratory, Robin lacking a sister and she a brother; certainly nothing to cause more than giggles, much less injury; yet child's play for all that.

'Yes, Dr Shanks. The actual path report'll be several days yet, but we can confirm negative on semen and negative on venereal infection. The vaginal swab did show positive, however, on some sort of cream. Not Snow's usual Vaseline, but an emollient with probable lanolin base. Tiny trace, of course, but we're sending it on to the Home Office lab to try and isolate it.'

'You're leaving it a bit late for the charge, Copper. Twenty-three hours, forty minutes you've had me in here now. In difficulties, are you? Kiddie remembered about that little fall she had on the fence, has she?'

Taff Roberts had noticed how, over successive arrests, Snow increasingly relished these little wind-ups, speculating on the weakness of the police evidence against him and mocking their efforts. It was a bizarre ritual, enacted with the relish of an Olivier, yet always for the same dour audience: the DI, his assistant operating the tape-recorder, and the solicitor, silent and non-committal as ever in his corner. Well, tough, you bastard, we've got a nice little shock in store for you this time!

Taff resisted the urge to hit him with it just yet, however; instead working steadily through the man's account of the meeting at the circus, testing him for inconsistencies which experience told him he wouldn't find, loathing his lanky, snake-like physical presence as much as his sneering manner, needled beneath his calm exterior by the man's sly, know-all taunting.

'And your interest in little girls like Vicky Bates – you attribute this solely to what you yesterday termed, er, parental fondness for children?'

'Also,' Snow affirmed, pointing at him with a sudden show almost of sorrow, 'also, to be fully honest with you, loneliness. I find myself increasingly at odds with the alienation of the modern world, cynical and cruel, like, and as a result drawn towards the gentle innocence of children.'

'Simply that, Mr Snow? Exclusively a, er, social attraction?' Taff could see from the narrowed eyes that Snow had guessed full well where this was leading but equally that it didn't seem to worry him.

'Social and parental, yes, Inspector.'

'So how do you account for the presence of these photographs found today hidden away in the garage you use for a workshop?'

To his surprise, Snow took and examined the photos, ignoring his solicitor's warning not to fingerprint them.

'It's okay, Mr Lisle, nothing to be ashamed of, whatever crude insinuations this detective may see in them.' He shook his head, baring his pointed yellow teeth at Taff as he passed the photos across to the solicitor. 'Art poses was how the gent described them in his ad. But I suppose someone with a warped mind – like say, a copper in charge of indecency crimes such as rape and sodomy and all that – might interpret them as sexually provocative. All down to your attitude, really.'

Jeremy Harris paused from checking his quarterly budget reports to lift and grunt into the telephone.

'Sorry, Mr Harris, but it's Inspector Roberts.' Then, resorting to a hammy version of Taff's Welsh accent, she added: 'Somewhat pressing, look you, boyo.'

'Thanks, Mary.' Pause for clicks. 'Hello, Inspector.'

'Thought you'd like to know, we discovered a nice little windfall: dozen pornographic pædi-pics hidden at Snow's place.'

'How did he react to that?'

'Phoney casual, wouldn't you know. But it was obvious Mr Lisle didn't think he had anything to laugh about.'

The CPS chief gave a cautious grunt, aware that Snow's was probably the more realistic evaluation since the photos were likely to be ruled inadmissible.

'Anything from Doc Shanks yet?'

'He says to expect much as before.'

'And how about the Bates family?'

'Angry enough to see it through, so Constable Hobbs reckoned.'

'I see.' Harris paused, weighing it all up like a grocer with his scales. 'So you're ready to go on indecent assault?'

'Too right we are. Remand in custody and strongly resist Mr Lisle's bail plea in the morning.'

Radio Marlbury has confirmed that local police now have a suspect in custody following yet another sexual assault on a child – this time an eight-year-old girl at the circus ground on Box Common yesterday lunch-time. The suspect, a man of 29 believed to be a resident of the Cressland Estate, is due to face magistrates in Marlbury court tomorrow morning charged with indecent assault.

At a press briefing earlier today, Divisional Superintendent John Leason confirmed that the child, a pupil at the nearby Box Common Primary School, was allowed home to her parents after medical examination and treatment. However, Superintendent Leason was unable, under the reporting restrictions on minors, to reveal the child's name.

Commenting on this latest assault – the third such this year, all on girls of less than ten years old – Labour Councillor Heather McGowan told Radio Marlbury: 'The frequency of these attacks is rocketing, regardless of the efforts of the police, the Neighbourhood Watch Committee and individual members of the public. Each time the police have nicked a suspect; each time in vain. Changes are needed in the law if the children and parents of Marlbury are to be freed from this lurking terror.'

Jenny Harris heard Jeremy's car as the news flash ended. It soured the mood of her greeting as she went out to him at the garage.

'That devil Snow again? They just had a report on the radio.'

'Again,' Jeremy confirmed, exchanging a perfunctory kiss before leaning into the rear of the Rover for his canvas briefs-bag. He had been all set with a rebuke of Jenny's Norfolk-weekend subversion and the way she was making use of Carry lately. Yet, inevitably, this latest Snow offence had to take precedence. Whereas their four-bedroomed 'character house' was situated a comfortable distance from the featureless estates of new-town Marlbury, the aura of fear reached out to their plushy suburb and beyond. The adjacent fields and woodlands, footpaths and bridleways, could no longer be regarded as safe. The activities of Carry and her friends, be it dog-walking, pony-hacking or even just visiting along the road, had to be constantly supervised.

'At least we know the monster's safely behind bars for a while.'

'Ah – well, maybe. Could depend on who hears his bail application tomorrow morning.'

'They *can't* let him out – surely!'

Jeremy Harris delayed his answer until he was in possession of a large sherry, its amber glow easing the tensions of the day. The sundowner habit, although lately up to two glasses per evening, had the added merits of ensuring that, on most weekday evenings, he actually talked to his wife, also that he ventilated the anxieties of the day, doing so at a level which was more personal and intimate than was possible in the office where, as chief, he had to remain somewhat remote.

'He has a basic right to bail. The onus is on us to establish why the bench should not release him.'

'It's obvious he'll simply go and do it again!'

'Most likely, yes. The difficulty is that he's only had the two previous convictions. None of his prior arrests can be mentioned – only those two. So it's a bit tricky to establish that risk.'

'Except they'll know – the magistrates – they'll have seen him in court on sex charges umpteen times before!'

'It doesn't follow they'll keep him in.'

'Blooming sure I would!'

'You haven't had their training – heard the Lord Chancellor's litany on bail hearings over and over.'

'In the opinion of most of the local mums, they're a bunch of softies.'

'Ha. *Used* to be. Over the last few years, thanks to the dissolute habits of Leonard Arthur Snow, the Marlbury Bench has swung over to join the hang-em-and-flog-em brigade.'

'Well, I'm sorry, but they haven't swung far enough to stop him.'

Suddenly there were pressing things for her to do in the kitchen; and Jeremy was left with all those things unsaid which he had needed to say – things like how very isolated these Snow cases always made him feel, having to stay remote and calculating while the police over-reacted and the public bayed in outrage . . . the grocer with his scales of justice, left alone with the decision that, once the investigation was completed, would be his and his alone to make.

Chapter Four

'You know the routine by now, Mr Lisle: not guilty, apply for bail and go for the Crown Court trial.'

'As before, yes.'

The solicitor rarely smoked. But right now, sitting with Snow in the holding cell at Marlbury police station, he wished he had a packet and could light up – less for his own gratification so much as to needle his cocky, gum-chewing client. It was a childish whim; yet, try as he might, each successive arrest brought on this urge to, at the very least, bring the yapper down a peg or two.

'You're sure about going for the full jury trial?'

'You should worry,' Snow smirked, 'it's all the more fees for you.'

'I'm not short of cases, thank you.' Then, examining his fingernails as an alternative to looking at his client, he added: 'Given the strength of your case and the listing delays to get into the Crown Court, you'd be best advised to let the magistrates hear your case and get it over with.'

'No chance,' Snow snorted. 'There's no way I'd get an unbiased hearing from a bench in this town.'

'You could end up being remanded inside for months.'

It was a minuet they always danced their way through, Lisle knowing the outcome yet obstinately insisting on going through the same familiar steps.

'Except, as you say, guv'nor, I have a strong case. Your brilliant advocacy'll have me out on bail, if not today, certainly in a week or so. I'd rather put up with a short remand inside than the rough justice in *this* court.'

'Yes, well, regarding bail, we might be best to delay the application until the next remand hearing.'

'Oh aye?' Snow drawled. 'Know something that I don't, do you?'

'As you very well know by now, if today's bench reject your application . . .'

'There's chambers.'

'. . . then you can *only* reapply here,' the solicitor persisted, quietly ignoring the interruption, 'in the event of changed circumstances.'

'Right.' Snow nodded confidently. 'Such as a weakening of the prosecution case – such as the withdrawal of their chief witness, namely, that confused little girl Victoria Bates.'

'It's your gamble,' Lisle snapped, disgust for once getting the better of him.

'If you're a betting man, guv'nor,' Snow grinned, 'I'll be happy to stake a tenner on it.'

The solicitor was spared further taunts by the rap on the door, a constable duly looking in to inform them they would be on in number one court, their hearing listed for just as soon as the bench had got the licensing applications dealt with.

'Who's chairman?' Snow called after the officer.

'Mrs Henderson-Grey.'

'There you are, then,' Snow crowed once they were alone again, 'piece of cake. You should have me home for lunch, no sweat.' Then, as Lisle started to gather up his case papers, jaw tight and eyes expressionless, the prisoner added: 'Oh, and this time, don't forget to apply for advance disclosure of their evidence.'

'Naturally.' The solicitor paused with quiet satisfaction in the doorway. 'I shouldn't be too hopeful of bail if I were you. Court one means we'll be up against the chief prosecutor.'

'What's this, Jemmy? Mohammed descending into the market place for a mere bail application?'

The CPS chief grinned uncomfortably, wishing that just occasionally Megan Hills could be a shade less outspoken.

'Your fault, Megan. Since you let your reckless driving run into a second day, I simply had to forsake my desk.'

It was true: he would have preferred her to take the case – partly because of her experience and seniority but also because it had been Megan who had succeeded in nailing Snow with both his previous convictions.

'Nonsense,' she insisted, 'you're here because you're afraid some less scrupulous member of your team might just bend the rules so as to get Snow off the streets. Blot, blot.' Megan allowed him a teasing Aussie grin before moving off to court three. Yet the sting was there just the same to prick his ego: the implication that at times he could be more lawyer than person.

'Your Worships, the prosecution emphatically oppose Leonard Snow's release from custody. Whereas indecent assault of a child is an either-way offence, it is none the less a very serious crime. Nor is there any need, I'm sure, to remind you that this is by no means the first such case in Marlbury. Indeed, the spate of such crimes is currently driving local parents to somewhat of a siege mentality.'

Whereas Jeremy Harris knew he was coming it a bit strong, he calculated he could go a good deal further than this before old Denny Lisle started clearing his throat in protest. The risk today, ironically, was of going over the top with this particular bench – or, more specifically, with this lady chairperson. As an Open University tutor in Sociology, Mrs Henderson-Grey prided herself as a defender of the underdog. Indeed, Harris had already decided to discount H-G as a lost cause and instead target his case at her two wingers, both as it happened men, one with sufficient years as a JP not to let the lady browbeat him. Hence the prosecutor's choice of the generic *Your Worships* rather than the individual *Madam*, to which he knew Lisle would resort. Also he spoke to whichever winger he could get eye contact with, largely neglecting H-G in the middle.

'As my friend will wish to remind you later, to withhold bail, you need to be satisfied on at least one of several principles: the risk that Leonard Snow might abscond so as to escape trial; the risk that, once freed on bail, he might yield to the temptation of committing further such offences; the risk that, once at liberty, he might attempt to intimidate witnesses – in this instance a couple of eight-year-old school-girls – doing so, moreover, in a situation where the local police need a lot more time to complete their inquiries.

'In addition to all this, Your Worships, there is the consideration of possible physical assaults on the accused himself due to the strength of public antagonism aroused by this spate of sexual offences.

'Whereas the prosecution acknowledges that Mr Snow has never breached bail on any of his many previous – ' Harris paused, inclining his head in acknowledgement of Lisle's grunt – 'er, on any previous occasion, Your Worships may feel that the second principle – the risk of further sex offences once released – is here a very real threat. He does have previous convictions for like offences. You may agree that in view of these and also the current spate of indecent assaults, bail could indeed be seen as, er, contrary to the interests of other potential child victims.'

Harris bowed and conceded the stage to the defence.

Denis Lisle's manner in addressing the bench was one of polite detachment, neither unctuous nor casual but so businesslike as to give the impression almost of shorthand – a style carefully fashioned for its appeal to the more seasoned and hence influential magistrates. Laymen they might be, he seemed to imply, but of ample experience to be treated as professionals with no time for flourishes or overstatement.

'No need to remind you and your colleagues, madam, of the defendant's *right* to be released on bail . . . simply to dispose of the arguments raised by my friend, albeit with certain liberties . . . Whatever the climate of local hysteria regarding similar recent offences, my client is *not* charged with those but *only* with an alleged assault on this one child, who evidently sustained no physical ill-effects since she was allowed to return home the same day. My client most strenuously denies the charge and will plead not guilty when and if finally committed for trial . . . I say *if*, madam, since it appears the prosecution case is based on somewhat tenuous evidence – in essence, my client's word versus that of his alleged eight-year-old victim.

'As to the prosecution's reference to previous convictions, you will see from the police sheet that his initial offence, for which he received probation seven years ago, may be fairly regarded as spent; while the second, three years ago, on which sentence was suspended, was for the lesser charge of common assault. A record, yes, but hardly indicative of a compulsive offender likely to rush out and reoffend the moment you grant him his freedom.

'Regarding my friend's suggestion of some sort of physical threat to the accused himself, Mr Snow points out that, in the event of any such threat from a lunatic element, he would sooner face it at home where he could then be sure of protecting his wife and toddler . . . a close-knit and loving family which, incidentally, Your Worships, represents a *de facto* surety against my client's absconding. He is prepared to abide by any reasonable bail conditions the bench may see fit to impose – passport, reporting, even a curfew – but, madam, since my friend has not offered absconding as a serious risk, the imposition of conditions would seem to be unduly oppressive . . . as indeed would be the withholding of bail prior to a Crown Court hearing which could involve a delay of several months before being listed for trial.'

He paused to bob the Chair a quick half-bow. 'Madam, unless I can assist you further?'

He remained standing expectantly while H-G exchanged a brief murmur with her colleagues. 'Thank you, no, Mr Lisle. But, Mr Harris, we would like to hear from you on the strength of the prosecution evidence.'

'Madam, yes.' The prosecutor stood up, sifting through his papers as a ploy to marshalling his reply. 'Your Worships, my friend is in error. It is not solely his client's word versus that of his young victim. The prosecution have a corroborative witness, the victim's schoolmate. Moreover, we anticipate expert medical and forensic evidence to confirm a sexual assault. Further to all this, material has been found concealed at the accused's home suggesting an avid interest in child pornography . . .' He paused, glancing round with a show of surprise as Lisle bobbed up in objection.

'With respect, madam, hardly that.'

'You have the material here in court, Mr Harris?'

'Madam, yes.' He handed the photos to the court usher who, after taking them for Lisle to check, handed them to the court clerk, who in turn briefly examined them before standing as he turned to hand them to the bench.

'I should point out, madam, the doubtful admissibility of these as evidence.'

Mrs Henderson-Grey nodded, glancing at the prosecutor as she gathered up her notes. 'If you've nothing further to add, Mr Harris, we shall retire.'

Tim Adams, as a grandparent and retired schoolmaster, had no doubts in his mind but that the menace must be kept safely locked away. The problem to which he applied his thoughts while the three of them waited for the kettle to boil prior to their discussion, was how to win over young Henry Johnson. He knew the man was an engineer of some kind with a couple of years on the bench, probably a family man and 'common sense' type by his looks; in any event, unlikely to welcome madam's bossy-boots style. So probably the more Tim could provoke H-G to her dictatorial worst the better.

'There's no doubt he's a weirdo,' he remarked, handing the photos across for Johnson to look at.

'Now then, Tim, don't let's start off with prejudices like that.'

'Just a straight comment, Hilary. Take a look at them. He's obviously a rampant pædo.'

'Whether he is or not, you heard what the clerk said about their admissibility.'

'For a jury trial maybe, but . . .'

'But nothing,' H-G retaliated keenly. 'What's at stake here is the man's liberty for, as his lawyer said, quite probably several months' wait in the Crown Court queue. That – ' she waved her hands to subdue his reply – 'no, let me finish – that long in prison, whether or not he's found guilty at the end of it all, is a longer sentence than he'd be likely to get even if convicted. Where's the justice in that?'

'It's entirely *his* choice. He doesn't have to insist on being tried in the Crown Court with all its delays.'

'It's still his right to choose. Besides, he'd be potty to face a bench in Marlbury where the entire bench know about him.' Hilary checked, flapping her hands in irritation, her fine litmus skin shading up as she turned to the silent Henry. 'Ignore that last remark, Mr Johnson. We don't *all* know him. And even if we do, it's not something we should allow *in any way* to influence our decision on his bail.'

'Excuse me, Hilary my love,' Tim Adams interposed, 'but there is no way I for one can possibly ignore that fact, and I don't see how we can possibly expect Henry to do so either.'

'Do at least *try* to stick to the proper . . .'

'Look, sorry,' the teacher persisted, 'but the police know it's him, *we* know it's him. I dare say half the little girls in Marlbury know it's him. So far as I'm concerned, that's reason enough.' He turned, all but knocking the coffee cup from Henry's hands. 'How about you?'

'No,' Hilary insisted sharply, 'we must give this the proper consideration.'

'Like what?'

'For a start,' she huffed, leafing through her court book, 'I'm going to read you the Lord Chancellor's guidelines.'

'We've heard them already – from both lawyers. Risk of absconding, of reoffending, of, er, ha, excuse me, of interfering with the little girl witnesses. Also seriousness of the offence – which this is.' Then, topping the chairwoman's further objection, he added: 'Listen, what I've always remembered is how His Honour Judge Brompton put it at our swearing-in ceremony. "I have no doubt," he told us, "that by and large you will reach the *right* verdict but often for all the *wrong* reasons."' Tim turned again to the silent junior winger. 'How about it, Henry? It's obvious to me what's right for that bastard out there, even if it's wrong by Hilary's precious guidelines.'

Hilary Henderson-Grey, flushed by now to an even deeper colour, was shaking her head, in despair as much of his assault on her authority as of his abuse of the judicial process. However, she stayed silent long enough for it to go to a vote, watching as Henry Johnson stubbed out his cigarette and drained his coffee before nodding in sombre resolve as he glanced at his male colleague. 'Okay then,' he said, 'for all the wrong reasons.'

'Leonard Snow, since your case cannot be heard today, you will be remanded in custody until the morning of the twenty-third of this month. The court is not granting you bail because we believe you would commit an offence while on bail, also that you would, er, threaten prosecution witnesses.'

If Snow was surprised, he gave no sign, his eyes narrow slits in the angular, pointed face, his long fingers drumming lightly on the edge of the dock.

'Our reasons are that you are charged with a serious offence and will face a heavy punishment if found guilty; moreover, that your character and previous record are not good. Therefore you will stay in custody until the twenty-third. However, should you wish, you have a right to apply for bail to the Crown Court. That is all. Take him down, Officer.'

'What's this I hear from the clerk in number one court about our esteemed Obersturmführer going over the top?'

Jeremy Harris glanced up from where he was still juggling the blessed budget reports. He would have liked to confess to his alarm on hearing himself, as she put it, going over the top – telling the bench by implication and default that Snow's guilt and past habits warranted his remand in prison – behaving more like an over-zealous junior than a branch chief.

'Megan, you're the one who said we didn't want him back on the streets.'

It worried him, too, that she gave him her Aussie grin, nodding in a conspiratorial way, as if to welcome him into some club from which his seniority had previously excluded him.

'I did you an injustice,' she chuckled, moving to sit opposite his desk. 'It wasn't our colleagues' integrity you doubted but their competence. Anyway, bully for you.'

'Lisle would have been wiser to hold off until the police have completed and also the heat's gone out of it a bit.'

'By which time,' Megan nodded in rueful agreement,

'to judge from past experience, your case could also be on the blink.'

Jeremy shook his head as she offered him a peppermint, then watched as she chomped one to a pulp with her fine white teeth.

'How high are you rating the evidence so far?'

'Assuming we get both little girls into court – well, we *might* – also that Doc Shanks has got over his Cleveland jitters, also that the judge allows those photographs – well, he *might* – I'd say we should be all right.'

'A lot of *ifs*.'

'Always are with the abominable Snow.'

'Good afternoon, Mrs Bates. Do you mind if I come in for a while?'

'Depends what you want.'

Janet Heanley forced a smile, by no means surprised by the woman's reticence. Pride counted for a lot on the Box Common housing estate and a visit from a social worker rated little higher than one from the police. Already she had detected the hurried sideways glances to see if either neighbour was about.

'Partly to see how wee Vicky's faring.'

'Well as might be expected.' The mother still made no move to let her in.

'Also, Mrs Bates, to discuss the implications following the incident.'

'The whats?'

It wasn't just reticence, Janet realized, but open resentment. 'For instance, to inform you of the case conference tomorrow. Also to offer support.'

'We can manage.' Then, with suspicion: 'What conference?'

Janet glanced pointedly to where the awesome Mrs Flynn had now appeared at the front window next door. 'If you want the street to hear about it, fair enough.'

She did not, of course, was already shifting dourly aside to gesture her hurriedly in. Once the door was closed, however, there were no further concessions, the woman standing, arms akimbo and chin out as she waited for the explanation. The home, from what Janet could see of it from the hallway, was reasonable for a working mother. She had seen a great deal worse than this in her time – smelt worse, too, for all the stale tang of cigarettes.

'Is Vicky not home?' Janet could hear from the TV racket that she probably was.

'That's for me to decide. Now what's this about a conference?'

'A child-abuse conference to review the case and decide what action, if any, may be necessary.'

'Eh?' The smokes were out now. 'What action?'

'To decide if she's to go on the register. To review if there's a need for supervision or follow-up.'

'I told you already, we can manage.'

'Fine.' Janet pulled out a pad and scribbled a note. 'I'll pass that view on for you at the conference.'

'Be better if you just forget the whole idea.'

'Impossible.' Then, overriding the mother's reply: 'Mrs Bates, unpleasant though it is, your daughter's the victim of a sexual assault. A shocking experience for her and also now the subject of a criminal prosecution. Several agencies involved – school, hospital, police, social services – besides just you as a family.'

'All right then, all right.' The woman was waving her hands in resignation. 'Where and when?'

'Tomorrow afternoon at the social services office. I'll be round afterwards to tell you of the outcome.'

'I'll be there, Miss Whatever your name is, don't you worry.'

'You'll be welcome at the department, of course, but not, I'm afraid, to attend the conference.'

'Why not?'

'It's confidential.'

'A meeting about my eldest girl – if she's to go on some bloody register or whatever – and we're not allowed to hear how or why?'

'Full details afterwards.'

'Oh no. I want to be sure and have my say. I know what you people can be like. Had enough of that when my husband was out of work last year.'

'Procedure, Mrs Bates, I'm sorry.' The protest was by no means new to Janet. Few parents accepted with equanimity. Yet, confidentiality apart, their very anger and emotions obliged their exclusion if objective decisions were to be achieved in the best interests of the child.

'Now then, about Vicky. You say, she's as well as can be expected. Will you enlarge on that, please?'

'Not to you.'

'Any after-effects – pain, shock reaction, distress?'

''Course there is.'

'Then I'll need details to pass on to the conference.'

'Tough.' She moved to open the front door for Janet to leave. 'If they want to know, I'll come and tell them.'

Chapter Five

'Why were you so long in the lavatory, Amanda?'

The girl stood by the teacher's desk, her face lowered in humiliation over her knotted hands.

'Was it because you missed register and assembly?' Silence. 'Well?'

Amanda finally managed a wriggle midway between a nod and a shrug.

'It's not like you to be late in the mornings, Amanda.' Pause for more wriggling, the child's pasty face unnaturally flushed. 'What happened?'

'Nothing, Miss.' The answer came in a quick gasp. 'Please.'

'Something made you late.' Pause. 'Where were you?'

The class was getting restless, the drama of interrogation now only partially holding their attention. The teacher turned to call for silence and, as a result, missed Amanda's whispered reply.

'Pardon, Amanda. I didn't hear you.'

'She said the circus, Miss!'

This brought on an immediate buzz of concern and speculation. Everyone knew what had happened to Vicky Bates at the circus ground – or rather, an increasingly lurid version was known – so the prospect of its now also having happened to Amanda prompted shrill comment.

'Be quiet! Five B, will you please all settle down!' The teacher was on her feet now. 'Is that correct, Amanda? Is that what you said?'

Whether it was or not, the girl repeated the wriggle, her face flushed more deeply than ever.

'Come along outside for a moment. Class, listen to me,

please: one sound while I'm outside and you'll all be in detention, understood?'

The teacher paused only briefly in the corridor, sufficient to put the one dreaded question. 'A man, was it, Amanda? Trouble from a man?'

'Yes, Miss.'

Detective-Inspector Roberts had his jaw clamped shut, his grip unusually tense on the steering-wheel. His grunt the previous day on hearing the magistrates' decision to refuse bail had concealed a surge of relief. It had been apparent to him from the chairwoman's tone that she personally disagreed. And Taff had acknowledged then that, for all his own certainty of Snow's guilt and the unexpected vigour of Harris's argument, bail had seemed more than likely. But now? Intercepted by a car-radio call on his way to see Lucy Morton's mother, diverted posthaste to the same primary school near the circus with a report of yet another incident?

'Hello, Amanda.' The nine-year-old didn't *look* like a hysteric any more than a wilful little liar; indeed, there was no denying the core of deep emotional distress in the child who, so the deputy head teacher had remarked when he hurried out to brief the detective in the corridor, was usually quiet and undemonstrative.

'What's this all about, eh?'

'It's me, you see. All my fault!'

Oops! Taff glanced up at Warren Green and also the school nurse. Both looked puzzled.

'Your fault with the man?'

'With Daddy, yes.'

'Daddy?' Double oops. 'How, Amanda?'

'It's because I'm so much trouble.'

For a moment, the detective eyed the deputy head, the latter raising his eyebrows and shaking his head in renewed bewilderment.

'You've tried to contact Amanda's parents?' Taff asked him.

'You won't find him,' the girl blurted out. 'Not now! Not after what happened this morning.' Her distress, intense though it was, manifested not in tears or incoherence; on the contrary, once started, she seemed anxious to unburden. 'Horrid, he was – horrid and beastly and rough.'

'Rough with you, Amanda?'

'What?'

'Your father – did he hurt you?'

'Me?' She shook her head in surprise. ''Course not!'

'You said he was rough.'

'*Yes*. Horrid and unfair!'

'Amanda, who was he rough with?'

She stared in confusion, her eyes switching to the nurse and then Mr Green. 'With Mummy, of course.'

'When?'

'This morning. Before he went away.' Then, her words punctuated with a series of small gasps, she continued: 'They didn't know, you see – not about me listening – hearing them – because they were shouting – on and on – and then hitting and things getting smashed and – and awful things before – before he went away – still shouting and-and-and then he bumped the car as he drove off.'

She broke off, huddling down into herself, appalled at this final outrage.

'Amanda, just to get it fully clear: your daddy wasn't rough with you? In fact, he didn't even know you were listening?'

'No! But it was my fault!'

'What was? You mean their row?'

'They wouldn't have all the worries about money and so on if it wasn't for *me*.'

Taff hesitated, knowing that the more he asked, the more tangled this web could become. 'And the circus?'

'I didn't go there. Honestly, I'd never. It was the others said that.'

'Others?'

'In class.'

'So your reason for being late to school . . . ?'

'I was trying to help Mummy. She was upset, you see. And she wanted to explain about Daddy. His job and all the worries. Except, I'd heard, you see, so I know he won't ever come back. Not ever again. *Never.*'

Charming community to live in, the detective reflected as he drove away from the school: job worries, domestic aggro, children at risk . . . Except that, hang it, he was seeing Marlbury not only through policeman's eyes but, worse, indecency-unit eyes . . . an occupational hazard guaranteed to distort society's ills out of all proportion since it was precisely those ills which he was paid to confront and deal with. Other people – the decent, healthy, law-abiding majority – got on with living their normal, decent lives largely unaware of the quirks, lusts and cruelty to which Taff Roberts was called. Unaware and untroubled, they were able to view their fellows with charity and affection, optimism and respect . . . in marked contrast to those officers lumbered with the chore of society's dirty washing.

'You were right to phone in,' he had assured the embarrassed Warren Green. 'The class teacher was right, too. Better a false alarm than an incident overlooked.'

Ironically, but for Leonard Snow and his reign of abuse, the Amanda alarm might well not have been raised – probably for the worse, since the child's catharsis had surely been a healthy release and now the pastoral teacher could contact the mother to offer help.

Inspector Roberts was not by choice a moralist or a puritan. True, his Welsh-valley upbringing, son of a Chapel deacon, had set him apart from his erstwhile colleagues in the Metropolitan force. The thought of taking a bribe to influence a case was as alien to Taff Roberts as the suggestion that the exalted captains of the City and the Establishment with their fat percentages and insider dealings should be in any sense immune to the laws which governed the less privileged and uninfluential. However, Welsh Chapel and democrat though he was, Taff had not been above living in sin for a few months with a divorcee media personality as a cohabitational try-out. Better to sin, after all, than to risk the multiple hash-ups, drink problems and aggravation which he had witnessed in the marriages of so many of his colleagues . . . hash-ups often reflecting that same copper's occupational hazard. You deal with dirt and violence and abuse, you risk accepting it as normal behaviour.

'Mrs Morton? Sorry to trouble you, madam. Inspector Roberts, Marlbury CID. I wonder if I might have a word about young Lucy's statement regarding the man we have in custody.'

'Nothing more to say. Sorry.'

Taff had known to expect a negative response after what Val Hobbs had reported to him. But for his determination to nail Snow, he would have accepted that he was unlikely to improve on the efforts of his able and experienced WPC.

'You see, madam, Constable Hobbs may not fully have clarified the situation when she spoke to you yesterday. The fact is, obtaining a conviction against a man like Snow is not easy. Vicky's evidence on its own won't be enough; nor will the medical evidence. To succeed – in other words to get this menace off the streets and away from little girls like Lucy – we need *all* the evidence possible, and that means . . .'

'No. Sorry.'

He had seen from the woman's closed expression that there was scant hope of getting her to reconsider. Yet it was worth the visit if only to plant the thought in her mind.

'I'll not pretend to you that having to stand up in court and point at the man would be easy for Lucy, but . . .'

'It ain't easy for her even having to go to school, mister, much less going to court. You any idea of the ragging and that she's caught there ever since? As for that there Vicky Bates – nothing but trouble, that little madam. I'd told Lucy before: you stay away from her, my girl, if you know what's good for you. Well, she didn't, and now she's learnt from her mistake.'

'Mrs Morton, I think . . .'

'She's highly strung, is that little girl of mine. Letting herself be led into all this by madam Vicky was bad enough without making it worse with school ragging and then courts and all. No. Sorry, but no.'

The best thing one could say about Marlbury prison was that, situated in the middle of the old part of the town, the redevelopment value of the site could be enormous. Yet even that was unsure since the Victorians had constructed their monstrosity in the heart of the ancient town which dated back to the Romans; so that prospective developers could face tedious archæological wrangles over such an historical site.

Since the 1960s Marlbury, like most of Her Majesty's county prisons, had been extended and adapted to a frantic extent to try and cope with the explosion in the prison population. Designed originally for a hundred or so Victorian felons, it currently contained over 450; and there was also a contingency plan to convert some of the disused workshops to a separate young-prisoners' wing. Few still pretended to the ideal of trying to rehabilitate inmates; far too costly, both in terms of staffing and facilities. Today's expediency was for maximum containment with minimum manpower, exercise and hygiene.

Visits to prisoners, for both convicted and remand men, were currently being compressed into a couple of linked Portakabins ingeniously fitted in just beyond reception – ingenious geometry but disastrous socially, the inmates and their families crammed at peak times chair-to-chair in a smoke-filled bedlam of rampaging kids and tense spouses for whom the gentle exchange of intimacies was virtually impossible.

Not that Sharon Snow expected much in the way of intimacies. Loyal wife and caring mother to his child though she was, the five years of their marriage had fostered no expectations of warmth. She had a far closer relationship with her mother-in-law than with her husband.

Now, having queued for half an hour outside with the increasingly restive Susan, having been searched and questioned, and having then waited for a further quarter-hour at their allotted table, she at last saw her husband ushered in by an escort officer. He saw her wave and started to thread his way between the crowded tables.

'You're late.'

'Sorry, Len. I never thought there'd be such a crowd.'

'Optimist, that's what you are.'

That he didn't kiss her was no surprise. However, he had plenty of affection for little Susan who had set up an instant clamour on seeing him. Secretly, Sharon envied the child the physical attention. But then, as she was often reminded, Len was just plain soppy about children, forever preferring their company to that of adults. The only exceptions to this were his fellow Civil War troopers; but then, to Sharon's way of thinking, they themselves were no more than a bunch of kids.

Undoubtedly, by indulging his fondness for children, her husband played slap into the hands of the vindictive local coppers. Their persecution of poor Len long predated her marriage to him. He had of course told her of it before their wedding; indeed, it was something she had accepted almost as a part of him, like a limp caused by some nasty accident as a youngster.

I made the mistake of giving the Fuzz some aggravation – waved two fingers at them when I got probation – and that was it: vendetta. Ten years' retaliation.

While waiting, she had bought them tea and chocolate biscuits from the WVS counter by the entrance. Now, sliding him his plastic cup, she asked if everything was all right with him.

'Situation normal, if that's what you mean.' He nodded towards a corner. 'Could do without *that*, though. Disgusting.'

That was a young couple engrossed in a passionate embrace in their corner. The woman, wearing a full-skirted cotton dress, had managed to manœuvre herself astride her boyfriend's lap in such a position that coitus was not only possible but, to judge from the inmate's response, actual.

'Imagine allowing that with all these kids around. You wonder society's morals is going to pot when they allow that sort of carry-on in public. Bleeding scandal.'

'Disgusting,' Sharon echoed, trying not to look. 'Whatever next.'

'And then they have the neck to refuse me bail on a trumped-up no-no of a case.'

'How could they, Len?!'

'Because they're all in it together, that's how. Police, lawyers, magistrates – all part of the conspiracy.'

'Justice, eh?'

It was a re-run of the scene they had often played out together. Yet, unlike Snow's lawyer, Sharon was blind to the irony, instead dutifully repeating her lines in response to the same old sentiments. 'Scandal, that's what.'

'Won't be long before I'm out, you'll see.'

'Yeah?'

'Crown can't go on lying about their evidence for long.

Few more days and we'll be applying to a judge for the out.'

'You should know by now,' the wife remarked artlessly.

'Damn right I should. Ought to sit for a law degree, all the training they give me at it.'

'You should, Len.' She nodded, her baby face twisting with a forced smile. Yet there was a thought nudging obstinately at the back of her mind which, like the motions of the couple enlocked in the corner, could not be ignored.

'Leonard . . .'

'Yeah?' The bleating tone of her voice alerted him, his eyes promptly slanting up from the toddler on his lap. 'What's the problem?'

'No problem. Well, perhaps it is, being as it's a new trick for them to pull.'

'Trick? What you on about?'

'Them – er – them photos – the ones the coppers planted down your workshed.'

'Ha.' His rhythmic gum-chewing resumed, his attention reverting once again to little Susan. 'As it happens, Sharon, that wasn't no plant.'

'You mean, you . . . ?'

'Forgot I'd stuck them away in there, as it happens. Meant to send them back, see.'

'But, Len . . .'

'A joke, Sharon, that's all they were.' The eyes flicked back in reproach. 'Some geezer in the troop – you know, that fat twit of a quartermaster – he sent them me as a joke, that's all.' Then, suddenly pointing a finger at her: 'Here, you never thought I'd go for stuff like that? Filth like that?'

'Course not, Len.' She looked away, avoiding the accusation in his eyes, her gaze reverting unconsciously to the corner where the coupling was now at a stage beyond which even the supervision officers could have stopped it – a climax enviously acknowledged with applause by inmates at a couple of nearby tables. "Course not.'

The Vicky Bates case conference, since the outcome was largely predictable, was under-attended, the list of ten apologies slightly exceeding those present. As the chairman, the local NSPCC officer, remarked: 'Whenever Snow falls, the salting team has to turn out regardless.' No one laughed: it was a standard pun for a routine event. Of those present, the educational people and the social services were noticeably more punctual than the medical staff or the police. Indeed, DI Roberts worked on at his desk until telephoned from the conference room, duly dashing across the corridor bridge linking the two office blocks and arriving breathless and harassed in time to catch the chairman's concluding remarks. No sign yet, he noticed, of the elusive Doc Shanks.

'We're here so as to consider putting Vicky's name on the register. Also the prospect of voluntary supervision or therapy and possible courtroom support,' the chairman summarized for Taff's benefit before nodding to Janet Heanley to take over.

'Mr Chairman, Dr Shanks's receptionist says she's chasing him.' Janet paused for wry effect; those who knew the lady receptionist in question smirked broadly. 'In the absence of both doctor and his report, I think it's in order to record that he gave me verbal confirmation of digital penetration. The usual, in fact. Unlike poor little May Bryant, young Vicky apparently offered no fight or resistance – which, as you can see for yourselves, is largely confirmed by Vicky's own statement. The opinion formed by WPC Hobbs and myself during the investigative interview was that Vicky's quite a cheeky and resilient wee girl, undoubtedly the prime mover over little friend Lucy Morton who sneaked off with her to the circus.

Lucy's rather mousy and precious, whereas Vicky's cocky by comparison. Quite the Len Snow "type" we might say; brash and vulnerable.'

The social worker paused for any queries and shuffled her notes before resuming. 'As I say, Vicky was either too confused or scared to offer any resistance. So she suffered no injury elsewhere and insufficient vaginal bruising to warrant a stay in hospital for observation. By the time she'd had all the Coke-and-cameras bit at Eckersley House, she was bobbing back up, fairly chirpy and articulate – provided, that is, that we kept her apart from her mother.'

Janet paused, pointedly gesturing her dislike for the benefit of those who hadn't met Mrs Bates, then grimaced as she caught the Inspector's eye. 'A difficult lady. Parks her youngest all day with a minder and her toddler in nursery school, so that me lady can work shift as a packer at Ventnors. She seems to expect far more of Vicky than her eight years would warrant. Certainly her first response before she knew the details was to blame poor Vicky for the incident. Uncooperative and obstructive towards me when I called yesterday after school hoping to see Vicky. Hostile and inclined to be anti-authority.'

This last was directed at the frowning Taff Roberts who was already scribbling a note of Janet's warning.

'I fear the prospects are not good for court, Inspector. Mrs Bates has managed to persuade herself and probably Vicky as well that she's been badly hit by the experience – shock, nightmares, what have you. I suspect that, whereas she's hard on the child in the normal course of events, she'll be all protective and anti about Vicky's giving evidence.'

Janet paused for a rueful shrug, then added: 'In the event that I continue as key worker on the case, I shall offer support in court. In fact, Inspector, you can offer her that from me when you see her. But I fear the omens are not good.'

'You haven't met Mr Bates yet?'

'No. And it may turn out he's more amenable than her. But, frankly, I'd be surprised. A very decided lady is Mrs Bates and none too pleased to be excluded from this little get-together, either.'

'From your tone, Janet, it sounds as though you'd be glad to have her excluded from Marlbury as well.'

'Not the most courteous of clients I've had to deal with,' the social worker confirmed. 'However, there are no grounds to suggest wee Vicky should be put on the at-risk register. The Bates family certainly aren't known to us or, I gather, to the probation or the police.' She glanced for confirmation at Taff, who shook his head. Whereas they had in fact found Mr Bates recorded on police files, it was only for some hooligan nonsense long spent.

'And from what you say, Janet,' the chairman put in, 'scant prospect of any voluntary supervision for Vicky, no matter how traumatic the Snow experience.'

'Scant indeed.'

They paused as Dr Shanks came puffing in with his usual over-worked-and-under-appreciated air, to bob in token apology to the chairman.

'Receptionist,' he murmured vaguely as he slid his report across to Taff. 'Managed to get this completed for you, anyway.' Then, turning to the gathering at large: 'Vaginal bruising consistent with digital penetration. Fairly positive on sexual abuse rather than this fall he's claiming she had. Labs may or may not confirm lubricant cream. Cautious devil that he is.' He turned to Janet. 'Any after-effects? The mother never brought her back for a check-up.'

'No? Well, that follows. As well as can be expected was how Mrs Bates put it. However, she implied there were after-effects.'

64

'Oh dear,' the doctor sighed, pulling out his appointments diary. 'Domiciliary then?'

'You can try.' Janet shrugged. 'Maybe it's just social workers she's anti.'

They turned as Warren Green intervened politely to the chairman. 'Er, I think Mrs Walton, Vicky's class teacher, may have something to add on Vicky.'

'Of course. Yes, Mrs Walton?'

'Yes, well, rather to our surprise, she was back at school the next day. Presumably because of her mother's going to work. Anyway, I had a quiet word, asked how she was feeling, suggested she stay off games and so on. She's certainly been pretty subdued in class – for Vicky, that is – during the last couple of days. But the teacher on break duty said she and little Lucy have been attracting a *lot* of attention in the playground. Inevitably, I suppose.'

'Well, it's all the rage,' the deputy head explained defensively. 'Sport of the week, right. You know what children are like about monsters and the forbidden. All the bully-boys playing Snow and hounding the squealing little victims around. A taste of the real thing, after all. Far more compelling than television. This actually happened. And Vicky's there to tell them how – again and again.'

'Fortunately,' Mrs Walton resumed, 'or perhaps unfortunately, Vicky's not one to shun attention. So the game is flourishing – along with misunderstandings and false alarms, Inspector, like we had this morning, calling you in to see poor Amanda Jenks.'

'Fair do's,' Taff grinned. 'Better safe than sorry.'

'And Vicky appears to be riding high?' the doctor asked, hoping to evade the home visit.

'A lot higher than wretched Lucy Morton, to all appearances.'

'From what you said, Mr Green,' Taff came in, 'it sounds as though another visit to your school by either me or WPC Hobbs would be timely. Give them the No Strangers pep-talk and so on.'

'The sooner the better,' Warren Green agreed, praying the head would back him, 'perhaps to the whole school, say, at assembly.'

'I'll liaise with your office later, okay?' Taff scribbled himself a reminder note, then turned to the doctor who was glancing pointedly at his watch. 'How would you feel if I came along on your home visit?'

'Frankly, unhappy. Why?'

'Miss Heanley reckons the mother may well oppose letting Vicky give evidence in court. Reassurances from you could help.'

Dr Shanks hesitated, cornered and drumming his fingers, aware of the attentions of the others – health visitor, welfare officer, school nurse, teachers, social workers – and the current move towards inter-agency cooperation. Yet, of them all, the medics had the strictest code of confidentiality to hide behind.

'Hardly proper,' he murmured. 'As a physician, I'm best to distance myself from the police.' Then, playing the Judas card to head off further response from the detective-inspector, he added: 'Anyway, I'm not sure I'd want to reassure any mother about her daughter giving evidence in a Crown Court. If it's a nightmare to me each time, how much more so to a little girl of eight, suddenly having to face the devil who had a go at her in the park?'

'I explained it all to them – how they'd all take their wigs and gowns off before she came into court, how Vicky wouldn't be sworn on oath, how she wouldn't be able to *see* Snow at all unless he stood up in the dock, how the judge would talk quietly to her like a big huggy-bear uncle and vet any tough cross-examination tactics by snappy lawyers. But no good, I simply couldn't budge them. Mr Bates even less than madam.'

'Oh dear.' Jeremy Harris was etching jagged red doodles on his blotter as he listened to the DI's gloomy news over the phone.

'Frankly, I got the feeling they're less concerned with sparing Vicky the ordeal than avoiding contact with authority.'

'Scared of being labelled as coppers' narks?'

'And betraying the estate code, yes.'

Harris could sense the policeman's bitterness. He was glad the fellow had decided to telephone rather than come into the office. Although he found the clean-cut Welshman pleasant and courteous, he sensed a certain reserve in his manner. Nothing personal, presumably, so much as the distance he had sensed from the police ever since the formation of the CPS had wrested responsibility for criminal prosecutions away from the crime fighters. All still members of the same team, perhaps, but with the CPS as the cautious and defensive backs at odds with the storming forwards line, impulsive and daring – and capable of being horribly wrong.

'There was a time when the code of that estate was rather different,' he remarked, attempting to elevate things to a more jocular level. 'In the old days, that is, when Box Common was part of the Lord Lieutenant's estates.'

No answering chuckle or even so much as a grunt; instead the Welsh voice persisted coldly: 'What I'm saying, sir, is that, on top of Doc Shanks's timidity, we now appear to have lost the evidence both of our victim and of her playmate. Boom-boom.'

'Well, I sympathize with the mother,' Jenny Harris remarked, bringing her husband a rather larger sherry than usual. To judge from his tensed state, he'd be needing extra to unwind. Yet, for all his frustration, Jenny could not compromise on the issue. 'Try and look at it from a parent's point of view, Jeremy. Would you want to push Caroline into giving evidence in a vast court, scores of adults, the whole pompous ritual?' Then, topping his retort: 'More to the point, what she'd *need* after suffering such a nightmare assault is help to forget it, have it all played down. Certainly not inflated into another ordeal. Probably a far worse ordeal in a way than the assault itself.'

'Well, yes, but . . .'

'Be honest, now, would you wish that on Caroline? Would you?'

'Of course not.' Tired and dispirited though he was, he could sense the force of her feelings on the issue; he realized, too, that they were spiced as ever with fear of the Snow menace, its grip now almost akin to a superstition. 'But if it had to be her ordeal versus Snow back on the streets . . .'

'But *why!*' Jenny checked herself, gesturing in apology. It was not their style to let fly at each other during the Happy Hour. 'I'm sorry, but I honestly don't see why it has to be endowed with all this procedure. Good Lord, if the Yanks can allow video links and taping of child victims to spare them the court ordeal, why can't *we?*'

'We're exploring the possibility,' he said, aware of the pomposity creeping into his tone.

'Exploring!' Again she gestured in apology. 'Sorry, but the Yanks are setting the style, breaking new territory, protecting the kids – thinking of justice for *them* first – putting the victim's rights above those of the callous offender. And meanwhile the Brits – worse, the pompous, hide-bound fee-grabbing legal brotherhood at the Bar – *explore* it! And no doubt in the end will pontificate against on the grounds that it's – I don't know – it's unconstitutional or something. Whereas, the fact is . . .'

'Let's have a refill of sherry, shall we?'

'Whereas, as it stands, the law's inept, slanted, chauvinistic and – and amounts to a virtual, whatsit, a groper's charter!'

'Correction,' the lawyer put in, glad in fact to find a point of agreement, 'a rapist's charter. Sexual assaults of the type Leonard Snow submits all these little girls to amount to rape, make no mistake about that, Jenny. And after today, I have to admit there's a sneaking prospect of his not being done even for indecency.'

Chapter Six

'Snags with the Snow evidence, Jemmy?'

'That depends.'

Harris's urge to air case worries with Megan was like a junkie's urge to share his habit and his shame with a fellow addict. Besides, since she would know the outcome as soon as it was resolved, there was no real indiscretion in confiding these latest reverses. The Rake's Progress, he reflected bitterly as she resumed.

'With the victim and her mate both no-nos, plus Doc Shanks getting a fit of the Cleveland jitters, *plus* an admissibility doubt over your Swedish porn-pics – frankly, cobber, your chances seem to be going heavily into reverse.' Then, spreading her tanned hands in apology at his evident desolation, she added: 'In fact, I'd say you're into injury time here with only one move open to you.'

The curious thing about Megan was that her plain-spoken, often brutal directness out of court was matched by a fancy and archaic turn of phrase in court . . . *respectfully request your Worships to let the mode of penalty reflect the woeful degree of turpitude ensuing from the offence* . . . as though, having adjusted to English law, she felt the need also to adjust her courtroom delivery.

'Plea bargain for common assault?' The prospect sickened Harris; yet Megan was right about going into reverse. 'Well at least it's old Denny Lisle.'

'Lord knows why he sticks by Snow. Wouldn't get me defending that evil snake for all the fees at the Bailey.'

Megan stood up, gathering her case files to leave. 'Want a bet on the outcome?'

'Hang it, Megan, no!'

Denis Lisle followed his tycoon client out of court two, spread his hands in bland apology and murmured that at least it was only a three-year disqualification. He was tempted to add that, if the client had left him to present the mitigation his own way, they might have got away with two years. Instead the tycoon had reckoned he knew better, insisting that Lisle alienate the bench with a lot of boring crut about how, as a captain of industry with umpteen jobs, contracts and exports totally dependent on his ability to drive di-dah-di-dah, when the bench very well knew that such a whizz-kid industrialist could very easily afford a chauffeur. It was a familiar dilemma to the lawyer, who also knew that, had he told the tycoon to pipe down, he would likely have lost him as a client which, since his partners also handled the contracts for his numerous companies, simply wasn't on.

'What about an appeal, Lisle?'

What about drinking less at lunch-time, the solicitor thought. Instead he suggested the client suffer two-year penance and then apply to the court for a review. It was with relief that he saw the branch crown prosecutor hovering for a word, bobbed in final unction and made his escape.

'Sorry to interrupt.'

'My pleasure.'

'It's about Snow.' With some defence solicitors, Harris would have been less direct, raising an irrelevance or two until finally reaching the indecency case as a by-the-by. 'I've now reviewed the evidence. The Crown might be prepared to scale down the charge to common assault if you can persuade your man to plead to that.'

A series of rapid assumptions clicked through the

methodical Lisle brain along with a feeling of mild regret. Winning for Snow was not something he relished. Yet that's how it looked if they were offering a deal: collapse in part if not in total. He shrugged, eyeing Harris dolefully. The prosecutor was not his favourite adversary: too much of a lawyer's lawyer, not human enough, too cold and calculating and career-conscious. Branch chief at under forty, hang it, and likely as not got his sights set on the DPP's office at the top of the dunghill. However, to be fair, Harris had put up a refreshingly unethical and spirited resistance to Snow's bail application, so maybe there was a heart in there somewhere.

'I'll put it to him, of course. In fact, I'll urge him to accept. Although no, on second thoughts, I suppose he's more likely to agree if I urge the opposite. Perverse customer.'

That his remarks implied a tacit acknowledgement of his client's guilt was something which caused neither lawyer any embarrassment. With the huge majority of cases Harris reviewed, the merits of the evidence were as academic to him as was the outcome of the trial. If he analysed them afterwards, it would be largely in terms of statistics – an attitude which was partially shared by Lisle. After all, the Crown and the individual client both had a right to have their case presented to optimum effect, in the latter instance, regardless of plea. So long as the client didn't confide his guilt or any prior intention of perjury, that was it: present and be damned.

'I must say, David, at times I don't envy you your job one bit.'

Taff Roberts fondled the sleek tabby cat on his lap and gave his landlady a wry grin. She was unashamedly fishing for indiscretions which he was just as unashamedly ready to divulge, Anne Cole being the nearest person he had to a confidant. Since confiding was vital when stuck with the gruesome job of Indecency, the landlady's sympathetic ear was the main reason Taff stayed on as her lodger instead of setting up a home of his own in one of the police-authority flats. Mrs Cole was, after all, probably as discreet a landlady as one could hope to find: a police-man's widow, her late husband gunned down while trying to tackle a gun freak on the rampage. No doubt whose side Annie Cole supported on the law-and-order front. No doubt, too, that she fancied her Welsh lodger rather more than was wise or prudent. For, given the deep scars of his recent affair with the ITN reporter, Kate Lewis, along with the physical turn-off of working on Indecency, Taff was doubly nervous of emotional involvement.

'At least the likes of Leonard Snow don't carry shooters,' he replied, 'although the psychological injuries they inflict on their young victims are likely to be no less devastating.'

'I was thinking of the responsibility,' she retorted. 'Suppose you're wrong. You've got this man Snow under arrest and locked away inside for what could be months, his poor wife and kiddie left alone to face a vicious hate campaign on the estate.' She paused, busying herself with pouring him a second cup of tea they both knew he didn't want. 'You must be terribly sure.'

Taff pulled a face, reluctant to confront the issue. Abruptly the cat jumped off his lap and went to sit by the door. Just why Anne Cole chose to play Devil's Advocate like this he couldn't fathom. As a bizarre antidote for the attraction she felt, perhaps, or even as a perverse trick to catch his attention?

'Listen, Annie, he's been identified by a score of little girls, all of whom had been assaulted sexually.'

'Little girls can be unreliable witnesses.'

'All right.' He nodded in concession. 'Confused, given to exaggeration and fantasy and pretence. We know all that. Which is why the interviews are conducted by specially trained people. The point is, on each occasion, Snow *admits* to meeting the child but denies the assault. Doubtless he'd argue that what he does to them is harmless and no more than a lot of them have had already from their elder brothers and stepfathers or have got coming to them shortly.'

He checked, embarrassed by the bitterness which had crept into his tone. 'Sorry.'

'What for? You go on. I asked in the first place.'

'Trouble is, you see, Snow's case has really got to me. Not entirely the man, vile though he is, but also the way the legal system virtually condones the act. The way it's slanted, you'd think it was a man's right to have his damned pleasure. Then, on top of that aspect, there's the officials who service the system: the police surgeon wetting his knickers in case he gets a mauling in the witness-box; the wimp of a prosecutor fussing on about the balance of evidence. What neither of them seems to care about is the public. We simply *have* to keep after Snow, even if we keep failing. We must hammer away at him with the toughest charges possible. The Force is getting slagged off enough as it is, what with having to act as virtual strike-breakers and so on. If we can't be seen as shielding local kiddies from animals like Snow, we might as well all pack it in and surrender to anarchy.'

'We've had an offer from the prosecution.'

'Tell me something new, Mr Lisle.' The only slight surprise to Snow was that it had come so early. Barely a week inside and already they were making offers. 'Common assault?'

'Correct.'

'Tell Harris to stuff it.'

'There could be some merit in it.'

'Yeah? Like what?' He unwrapped a stick of gum and put it in his mouth. 'Face a Marlbury bench like those prats the other day? You've got to be joking. About as much regard for rights and justice as a commissar in Siberia.'

'We could apply for the case to be heard by magistrates elsewhere – say, at the far end of the county.'

There was a brief pause, Snow staring at him with his cold, goaty eyes, so that for a moment Lisle thought the man was considering the offer's merits. Instead, jabbing a finger towards him, he remarked: 'You're telling me to plead guilty to something I never done, Mr Lisle. That can't be right, can it?' There was no hint of irony; the performance was as earnest as ever.

'You did so once before . . .'

'Ah well, that was my one mistake. That was before I learned. You advised me, Mr Lisle: innocent you may be, Mr Snow, you told me, but the balance of evidence is such that a jury could well find against you. Do a deal on common assault, even though you never done what they're saying, and you can be sure that the worst you'll get is a suspended sentence. Well, fair enough, you were right about the suspended but, with respect, you were dead wrong to advise the guilty plea for common. Look how that's stood against me ever since. Every bail application, up it comes: probation *and* suspended: oh dear, dear. Well I learned from that, guv'nor, learned the hard way.'

The lawyer went to speak, but his client was now in full spate.

'You'll notice the hurry they're in with their magnanimous offer. Just a few days ago in court that geezer Harris claiming this, that and the other: two witnesses, medical and forensic, filthy photos. Now suddenly he's horse-trading. You know why, don't you? So's he can get it away without advance disclosure of evidence, that's why. Once we've seen that, he knows he's got no cards to play. He's trying to bluff us, Mr Lisle. A gambler with a fistful of nothing, that's our Crown Prosecutor. So you just go and get him on the blower and tell him no deal. Then you get on to the Crown Court and fix to see a judge in chambers pronto. That way we'll call Harris's hand. Want to bet what he's got left to play, do you? 'Cos I've got a tenner says he's lost his two little girls and his police surgeon's bottling out and all he's got to go on is them Swedish art snaps.'

Status is size in the Civil Service, Harris reflected as he eyed the spacious accommodation awarded to the grade-five Chief Crown Prosecutor. The room was half as big again as his own grade-six BCP's office, whereas his team of fifteen senior and Crown prosecutors all had to share an open-plan office resembling the newsroom of a daily paper. The lawyers' desks, however, were far more generously spaced than on the floor above where the executive and administrative officers were packed in along with the typists and extensive filing system.

Apart from his splendid grade-five desk, three chairs, security cabinet and potted orange tree, the CCP's large room was empty. Rarefied space for his rarefied thoughts, perhaps. Certainly Tony Berrington did his personal best to fill the room, being not only large in his person but in his gesture, his laugh and his manner.

So far the weekly CCP-BCP meeting had gone routinely enough, the pair disposing of Harris's under-staffing and use of agency lawyers, also of one domestic murder, a couple of GBHs and a potentially tricky batch of riotous assemblies, all without discord.

'I see you've copped Snow on another indecency,' Berrington remarked mildly, his eyes on the list. 'Prospects?'

'Average to poor,' Harris confessed.

'And not greatly helped by this.' The CCP handed

across the MP's letter which the Director's office in London had forwarded to him that morning.

Monty Carlaw, Hon. Tory Member for Marlbury, was no friend of Jeremy Harris. The dislike was rooted in the essential independence of the judiciary from politics. Parliament might frame the laws, but their interpretation and application was the jealously guarded role of the judiciary, of which the Crown Prosecution Service was the front line. Hence, opportunist MPs like Carlaw, seeking to exploit public sensitivity over notorious cases like Snow's, were even more of a pain than the local press.

The letter, a rehash of one he sent each time Snow was arrested, began with a pious nod to the constitution '. . . *not, of course, for politicians to attempt to influence matters of jurisprudence. None the less, public debate over recent controversial prosecutions and light sentences relating, in particular, to sexual offences prompts some cautionary observations regarding the case of Leonard Snow, currently charged with indecently assaulting a girl of eight in my constituency . . . draw your attention to the extensive lobby, both in the press and also at community level through PTA and Neighbourhood Watch committees, alarmed at the persistency of such offences in Marlbury . . . incumbent on me as their elected representative in Parliament to urge the Director of Public Prosecutions to review this case so as to ensure that the charge pressed is of appropriate severity . . . abundantly clear to me from letters, petitions and attendance at my weekly surgery in the constituency that anxieties over the risk to local children will persist until this menace is finally brought to book . . .'*

'I'll send the director a background note,' Jeremy promised, slipping the letter into the case file.

'So where's the problem? Indecent assault's the realistic maximum on the facts.'

'Except, as of yesterday, I hinted at common assault.'

'Ah.' The CCP commenced the rigmarole of filling his pipe. 'Collapse of witnesses?'

Harris gave a rueful nod.

'Oh dear.' The chief sat back with a sigh, and Harris braced himself for the rebuke – ever so tactful and oblique, of course, but rebuke for all the polite phrasing. 'Entirely your decision, of course, brother. I know Carlaw's just playing politics, but his point about public sensitivity is valid. We're not elected, praise be. But equally we can't afford a total disregard of public sentiment. I'm fully aware of the guidelines but when all's said and done, that's all they are – a guide rather than hard-and-fast rules.'

Harris nodded solemnly, reaching for his coffee-cup as an excuse to avoid Berrington's searching gaze. Decisions in this area, so grey and non-specific, were his *bête noire*. He would have preferred them to be definite rules rather than discretionary, since they forced him into this no-win situation: press on with the full indecency charge and he would be courting humiliating defeat, but back down in accordance with the guidelines and there'd be a public outcry. It always seemed so unjust to Harris that whereas such outcries were born of public ignorance, London seemed inclined to side with them.

It was all so negative of the Director: Harris's branch could win a series of dazzling court victories and nothing would be heard from on high in acknowledgement; but prompt a public outcry over a sensitive case like this and rumblings of disapproval would reach him from Berrington . . . a nightmare for BCP Harris, the civil servant for whom Law was what mattered. Had image and PR been his forte, after all, he'd likely have been a defender instead.

'In any event, Tony, it's academic since, on past form, Snow's unlikely to buy the offer.'

'Ah.'

'Far more likely be going for bail in chambers and then an old-style committal.'

'Yes, well, who better to know his *modus operandi* by now than you, Jeremy.' Berrington paused to light the pipe, puffing smoke around the big, airy office. 'Anyhow, it's your decision, as I say.' He conceded a grin like a pat on the head. 'Have to admit, I'm glad it's not mine.'

They turned as his assistant came in with a message from Harris's office wondering if he could fit in a quick hearing with Judge Wallace at Reading Crown Court after he was finished with the CCP.

'Ah. And to be sure and take in Leonard Snow's file, I suspect.'

'How did you guess, sir, yes.'

Hugh Wallace turned from removing his wig, robes and bib; then, putting on his jacket and tie, he moved to sit at his desk opposite the two solicitors. He was a tall, once-athletic man who, even without his robes and wig, carried about him the presence of authority. It was not unmerited. For all his pleasure in stylish living, Judge Wallace had the brain to keep well up with developments in criminal law and way ahead of most counsel in court. It mattered: he was both respected and feared by those at the Bar: not a man to tangle with, in court or out. Sharp as a sword with comments and rulings; seldom wrong and never worth challenging even if he was. When in chambers like this, he was given to lay turns of phrase, as if to emphasize his familiarity with the ways and wiles of the common man. Nobody's fool, except perhaps his own; for he thought highly of himself.

'Bail withheld,' he read out from the Marlbury clerk's note, 'because the justices feared further offences and threats to prosecution witnesses.' He glanced wryly up at the two solicitors. 'Which, since the bench were bound

to have recognized chummy, was only to be expected.'
Then, as he again scanned the notes: 'Reasons, seriousness of offence, hence heavy punishment due; also bad
character and previous.' Again he glanced up. 'The latter
hardly so: his first offence spent, his second all of five
years back and suspended. Hardly amounts to bad
character in our book, eh, Mr Lisle?'

'Quite so, Judge.'

'Which, of course, totally disregards the fact that this
fellow Snow's been nabbed and held in custody time and
time again for banging these poor little girls, eh, Mr
Harris?'

'Correct, Your Honour.'

'Which is all very well for lay justices to act on in
Marlbury Magistrates Court but won't do for professional
lawyers like us, eh, Mr Lisle?'

'Correct, Judge.'

'That said, the justices were doubtless made aware of
the strength of the evidence against chummy, yes, Mr
Harris?'

'Indeed, sir.'

'Which at that early stage probably looked and sounded
a great deal more formidable than it does now.' The judge
sat back, easing his thumbs under his braces as he eyed
the prosecutor. 'All right then, what you got?'

He could see from Harris's tilted smile that it wasn't
worth much, and it disappointed him. He would have
liked nothing more than to have kept the sly little sex
freak banged up inside, less perhaps because of his quirky
habits so much as because he kept making a monkey out
of the august forces of law and order.

'I have to admit, sir, we appear at this stage to have
some difficulty with the medical evidence.'

'Difficulty?'

'I've known Dr Shanks to deliver more positive
observations.'

He slid the medical report across plus a copy to Lisle. The judge skimmed through it in seconds without missing a jot. It had Cleveland stamped all over it. He glanced up, pulled a sympathetic face, then asked: 'What about the little girl, Vicky Bates? Going to get her into the box?'

'Let's say we're working on it.'

'Meaning unlikely, so Mr Lisle will tell you.'

'Meaning we still have hopes,' the prosecutor blustered, wishing they'd got old Judge Handley instead of Pile-Driver Wallace. He thrust across Vicky's Section-nine statement, compiled with Val Hobbs at the Eckersley House interview. 'Positive and clear, Your Honour, for an eight-year-old.'

'Provided you can get her into court, Mr Harris. Provided.'

'Of course, sir, as always in child sex cases. But, with respect, that is not at issue yet.'

'Very well then. But what *is* at issue – indeed, what we are here to test – is whether there is evidence strong enough to deny a man his liberty – a man, moreover, who most strongly asserts his innocence. No matter what we may all three know or believe we know about that man and his habits, it is our role as paid professionals to review the evidence and reach a detached, objective decision, yea or nay.' He gestured in wry conclusion of this homily, then resumed to the prosecutor. 'What else?'

'Pornographic photographs found hidden at Snow's home.'

'Ah. Which our friend Mr Lisle doubtless submits must be ruled as inadmissible. Let's have a dekko, then.'

'I'm sorry, Your Honour, but they're in safe keeping with Marlbury CID. I came straight here from a meeting with Tony Berrington, so no chance to collect them.'

Judge Wallace pulled a face, then listened gloomily while the two solicitors haggled over possible interpretations – art versus suggestibility versus downright prurience – and finally he waved for silence.

'All right, I think I get the picture – or pictures – which, assuming Mr Branch Crown Prosecutor is not going to get his Vicky Bates into the box with any other corroboration, are clearly about all he's got left. And, listening to what you both said just now, it sounds to me as if, in balance, Mr Harris, you're on a loser.'

'Your Honour, I submit you should see this evidence. I can get it here in under an hour and . . .'

'Answer me one question, Mr Harris,' the judge interrupted politely. 'Have you in the last day or so made any informal overtures to Mr Lisle concerning the case?'

'With respect, sir, I submit that's a most improper issue to introduce.'

'Which I take to mean, yes, you have. Am I correct, Mr Lisle?'

'If it was informal, Judge, then I'd have to regard it also as confidential.'

'Which, again, I take to mean, yes, you have.' He snapped his thumbs out of the braces and leaned forward. 'Very well, gentlemen, enough expenditure of taxpayers' money. Your client will be released forthwith, Mr Lisle, subject to the following conditions: one, that he resides at an address not nearer than fifty miles from Marlbury. I recall he took his family to live with a relative in Wiltshire last time. Two, that he remains outside a fifty-mile radius of Marlbury unless required to return here for specified business relating to his trial, in which case he must be escorted by police or prison staff while in the Marlbury area. Three, that he report daily to the police station nearest to this Wiltshire residence. Four, that he surrenders his passport. We went into the matter of financial sureties last time, Mr Harris, and you bowed out, if I recall correctly.' He turned to Lisle, 'You have a note there of the Wiltshire name and address, I see.'

'Here, Judge, yes.'

'Very well then, gentlemen, Leonard Arthur Snow to be released on bail subject to those four conditions.'

Chapter Seven

Execution of Judge Wallace's bail order was complicated by virtue of the conditions. The movements officer at the prison insisted that, whereas Snow clearly had to be escorted beyond the specified fifty-mile limit, such was the staffing crisis at the prison that it could be several days before the necessary transport could be provided to get him there. Pressured by Lisle, the officer retorted that they were having problems enough producing prisoners under escort at court, much less, as he put it, acting as a taxi service for bailed nonces. Scandalous, retaliated Lisle: a man's liberty ordered by a judge but denied, or at least postponed, by bureaucratic ineptitude. Advised to take it up with the Home Office, the solicitor instead went back to the judge. Hugh Wallace promptly directed a blast at the prison governor, then listened with scant sympathy to the man's bleating about the militancy of the Prison Officers Association. Lumbered with the problem, the governor contacted the Marlbury police, pointing out that the judge had specified police as alternative escorts and reminding the station super of one or two favours owing. Superintendent Leason huffed and puffed about resource allocations but eventually agreed to assign a Ford Transit team.

Marlbury being a chatty sort of station, it followed that word of all this soon reached DI Roberts: *Snow not only released on bail, guv, but getting chauffeured around by the lads*. Taff, although he let fly some expletives, was not surprised by the man's release. In fact he went and located the two lads in question shortly before they were due to leave. Since both were resentful of the chore, the more senior of the two readily accepted the DI's offer to relieve him of the duty.

'You fancy the bastard's company all the way to Wiltshire, mate, that's fine by me. Just be sure you only put the boot in when George is watching the traffic.'

'That old prat Lisle did something to earn his fees for once, then,' Snow remarked on the drive away from the prison. 'The screws told me I'd got bail but how I couldn't get out 'cause of the fifty-mile condition. Now, surprise, surprise, old Denny's whistled up the fuzz.'

'Thing is,' Taff confided, 'we needed the cell space for another customer.'

'Oh yeah? What's he done?'

'Murder. Did his mother-in-law in with a flat-iron. We asked him why and he said she needed straightening out.'

Snow snorted, only to stare in suspicion as the detective offered him a stick of gum. 'What's your game? Think you're going to chat me up? Lure me into indiscretions?'

Taff shrugged, laying the gum where Snow could reach it if he wished. 'If you're innocent as you say, Mr Snow, you've nothing to fear.'

'Ha!' He nodded towards his home as the constable driver pulled up outside. 'Try saying that to my missus and see what she says.'

'Mrs Snow reckons you're innocent, Sunshine.'

'Right. But she's seen the aggro year after year. Less from you, I guess, being as you're only carrying on what you took over from that vindictive maniac, Hargreaves. But she's seen it all. She knows.'

Sharon Snow came out to the Transit, one hand clutching a suitcase, the other keeping a firm hold on toddler Susan. She was surprised to recognize the detective seated in the back beside her husband.

'You may think of this as a release for him,' she remarked sourly. 'All I can say is, you should try living with that sister of his and see if it's better than Marlbury nick.'

'No use complaining, Mrs Snow, being as a judge ordered it.'

'Oh yeah. Same as last time. Well, I hope you're satisfied, that's all. Hounding a family out of their home for weeks on end. Scandal, that's what.'

Her husband nodded in approval of her invective, reaching out to replace his spent gum with the fresh stick before moving forward to hoist the excited Susan into his arms.

'What if we was to pack up and move home, eh, copper?' the wife asked once they had loaded in the luggage and were heading for the motorway. 'Len says you lot'd just keep after us, no matter where we went. That right, is it?'

'Leave it go, Sharon,' the man cut in. 'Don't matter what he says, we both know there's no escape.'

'I got spat on the other day,' she burst out, the humiliation surging up in a plaintive cry. 'Spat on! And why?' She jabbed a finger at Taff. ''Cause of all the lies you mob keep spreading about him, that's why!'

Taff glanced briefly at her and, meeting the bitter indignation in her eyes, shook his head in denial. He would have liked to tell her, yes, leave the district, you and little Susy both; escape it all, but go without your sick pervert of a husband.

For all her hatred, he felt deeply sympathetic towards the wretched woman, less so for the betrayal of loyalty which she would one day have to endure, so much as for the anguish she would suffer sooner or later over her frail little daughter. For the expression in Snow's eyes as he held the giggling Susan tight on his lap left no doubt in Taff's mind as to the child's eventual destiny.

* * *

'There is no denying, unless the police can persuade Mr and Mrs Bates to reconsider their refusal to let their daughter give evidence at the trial, the prosecution case is not strong.'

Harris paused yet again from dictation to pace yet again around his grade-six office with its medium-sized desk and sickly rubber tree. Plaguing Members of Parliament! Of all his chores, he most resented these essential background notes to the DPP. They invoked memories of having to report to the house prefects as to why one was late for nets practice or, worse, had failed to fulfil one's fagging duties.

'Change *not strong* to, er, *seriously weakened*. Then go on: None the less, it is the Crown's intention to continue with the prosecution on the original charge of indecent assault. Paragraph. It is perhaps worthy of note that any element of possible injustice against the defendant vis-à-vis the latent weakness of the prosecution case has now been substantially vitiated by the decision of His Honour Judge Wallace to release Snow on bail, subject to reporting and residential conditions. Paragraph. Finally, the probable date for committal has been set for the twenty-second of next month, for which the defence has now requested attendance of all witnesses for an old-style committal. Hence, such evidence as the police have been able to muster will be fully tested on that occasion. Whereas the Crown will of course brief counsel, I have to record that, at this stage, the balance of probabilities rests somewhat in favour of the defendant.'

'A senseless breach of procedure, Roberts.' The superintendent rapped it out, refusing even to meet Taff's gaze. They had been back from Wiltshire barely an hour before the summons had come from the chief's office. 'The sort of macho nonsense I'd expect from an SPG ape, perhaps, but certainly not an officer of your rank and experience.'

'Sir.' Taff, although fuming that it had come to light, knew better than to retaliate too swiftly with a rule-book type like Leason.

'Whatever style you used to follow with the Met, you know by now that in the Thames Valley we do things by the book.'

'That's one reason I applied for the transfer, sir.'

'Well, then, whatever were you playing at, man? Investigating officer on the case, the prosecution already under way, defendant out on bail. Why ever go and flout the hands-off rule like that?'

'Impulse, I suppose, sir.'

'To what? Harass the man?' Then pre-empting the DI's reply: 'That's how his counsel will portray it at the trial. Procedural irregularity, exceeding authority, intent to harass and intimidate due to vindictiveness over the man's release on bail.'

'With respect, sir, I very much doubt the case will now proceed to trial.'

'Pardon?'

Taff shook his head in rueful frustration. 'Lost our witnesses, gone duff on the forensics. On past form, we can expect Mr Harris to chuck in the towel.'

'Hm.' Leason shook his clean-cut PR head in persisting reproach. 'Unduly defeatist, and certainly no justification for pushing into that Transit the way you did.'

'Sir.'

Pause, the station super smoothing the papers on his desk before glancing curtly up at his DI. 'Surely to God you didn't expect to trick him into an indiscretion?'

'A sly devil like him?' Taff snorted in rueful denial. 'In fact, his solicitor reckons Snow gets as much of a kick out of beating us at our own game as he does getting after all those poor little kiddies.'

'Damn it, Roberts, all the more reason to play it by the book!'

'Yes, sir, except – well, we may have lost this one, but we know there'll be another – and another – until we finally nail him. Okay, know your enemy: that's what I reckoned when I went along for the ride today.'

It was the chief's turn to snort, shaking his head in open derision. 'Spare me the Maigret nonsense, Roberts. You made a crass mistake, and I just hope for your sake nothing further comes of it. Now get out.'

'The fact is,' Taff persisted, standing his ground, 'I got more than I bargained for – witnessed a dimension of him I'd never expected to see.'

'Well?'

'I saw him with a *victim*, sir.' Then, his voice rising regardless of the other man's seniority: 'Never thought I'd feel the impulse to commit cold-blooded murder, but damn sure that's what I felt today, watching him sat in that Transit in possession of that innocent little daughter of his.'

'Gentlemen, the only sure thing about this case is my fee at the end of it.'

Edwina Prosser, counsel for the Crown, paused to draw heavily on her cigarette. It was the one manifestation of her nervousness in a situation which, if not routine, was certainly familiar to her: police coming on with a lot of pressure for PR reasons while the prosecutor sat on his hands and left the haggling entirely to her. The fact that the DI in question was extremely dishy and earnest and persuasive did not help Edwina, securely married and career-conscious as she was. One simply could *not* contemplate stray affairs, least of all with the Force.

Any why not let him have his way after all? For all the ignominy of defeat, it would mean a far fatter fee at the end of the case.

Nor was Edwina by nature a loser, far from it. First-class honours and now, after ten busy years at the Bar, possessed of a string of criminal scalps worthy of any Temple barrister. Yet she had known from the moment she first opened this brief and saw the indecency charge and the age of the victim that it was a challenge. More, after gauging the weakness of the prosecution evidence, she knew the worst.

'I understand they applied for the old-style committal even before being served with the evidence.'

'Yes, well, er, that's no more than a conceit on the part of the defendant.'

'Ah, but then he's a cell-block lawyer with rather more acquittals to his credit, as it were, than you've managed convictions.'

'As it were,' Jeremy Harris acknowledged dourly. Edwina's jokes tended to be on the mordant side.

'There's a lot of local feeling attaching to this case, madam.'

'I dare say, Inspector. But are you suggesting I should approach it in the manner of a crusade? Thunder in on my old white charger totally bereft of weapons?'

'No, ma'm.' Metaphor, Taff reflected, was no more her forte than humour. However, if her advocacy was half as good as her looks, they'd be in with a chance. 'There's his dirty pictures.'

'A cardboard sword, I fear. All right, I take your point that the Marlbury justices may overrule defence counsel's objections to those pictures, if only out of prurient curiosity. And it may just be that the pictures, plus local knowledge, could tip the balance our way for a committal to Crown Court. But frankly I wouldn't want to lay odds on that.' She gestured in apology, turning to the branch crown prosecutor. 'I take it you offered them common assault?'

Harris hesitated, wishing these London barristers would learn to be less outspoken in front of the Thames Valley Police. True, Roberts had been Met until a couple of years ago; but rumour had it that he'd quit over what amounted to a matter of honour. And in any event, it was galling to have to reveal his ill-advised overture to the defence.

'Informally, yes,' he muttered, avoiding the detective's gaze, 'when we lost both girls.'

'And rejected by which lawyer? Real or cell-block?'

'The latter, of course.' Not, Edwina reflected, that there was any realistic prospect of her jacking up a deal with Sam Mullins, Snow's counsel. No chance. After all, a plea of guilty to a lesser charge would occupy only a fraction of the court time listed for the contested committal, which would amount to a proposal that Mullins forfeit the major portion of his fee! Although the same fee loss would apply to Edwina, she was less worried by it, regarding this character Snow as somewhat of a long-term investment – a cherry from whom one could expect, as it were, many more bites in the future.

'Very well then, Jeremy, it's your decision. If you insist, then your lady knight will charge in armed with naught but her cardboard sword to satisfy the calls for blood of the Marlbury masses.'

As it turned out, very few of Marlbury's masses were present in court one for Snow's committal: the Tory MP's secretary, a member of the Neighbourhood Watch committee, and a couple of OAPs who made a regular Wednesday-morning outing of it regardless of what was listed. In the event, they and the three local court press reporters were all disappointed – but less so than defence counsel Mullins, since the Crown's intended line would after all chop his fee.

'Case number one on your list, Your Worships, Leonard Snow, listed for committal for trial in the Crown Court.'

Snow, seated this time in front of the dock instead of in

it, stood up in readiness, only to be waved down again by the clerk.

'Your Worships, I understand the Crown has an application to make in this case. Miss Prosser.'

Edwina stood up from beside the grim-faced Harris. She glanced briefly at Mullins, then bowed to the bench.

'Your Worships, the Crown finds it is no longer in a position to offer any evidence in this case. Accordingly, it asks for the charges to be withdrawn against Mr Snow.' She bobbed and sat down with as much dignity as she could raise in this undignified situation.

The decision, galling though it had been, was now something of a relief to Harris. Far from victory, their sole prospect had been one of mutilation at the hands of the able Mullins. Best by far to overrule the emotional DI and bow to the wisdom of counsel.

Studiously avoiding Snow's leer of triumph, he started to collect his papers as Sam Mullins stood with the inevitable application for costs. Aware in advance of the Crown's capitulation, he had got busy in advance with his calculator.

'In the event that Your Worships are minded to award costs out of central funds to the defendant, there would appear to be two courses open to you. I have here a calculation of £2500. Alternatively you may prefer to make a generalized order in the defendant's favour, the precise sum to be agreed later, subject to arbitration.'

The bench chose the latter course. And Leonard Snow left the court a free man, exonerated, exultant and laughing.

PART TWO

Chapter Eight

'That child's at risk, Miss Heanley. I'm telling you, I've *seen* Snow with her, and I'm convinced little Susy is definitely a target.'

It had grown to haunt Taff Roberts over the last month or so, ever since recognizing the lust in the man's narrowed eyes as he clutched the child in the van. Prior to that, the detective had merely disliked Snow, regarding him as a menace to be curbed. Having had to face in London the parade of cruelty and excess to which Metropolitan Police officers are daily exposed, the DI had become inured to barbarity; hence, on taking over the Indecency unit at Marlbury, he had lacked the excessive zeal of his predecessor. Now, however, the vulnerability of that deep-eyed toddler had sparked as a catalyst inside him. For here was one victim whose fate they could predict; worse, a victim who, for all her tender years, could well be exposed already to abuse. Whereas the legal technicalities had consistently undermined their efforts to nail Snow for his more random offences, at least protection of this little girl could be achieved with less cumbersome legal restraints.

'Take the child into care, you mean, Inspector?' Janet Heanley had never seen Susan Snow, indeed had only glimpsed the child's mother once during one of her husband's court hearings. 'We'd need definite grounds.' Then, overriding the policeman's retort: 'Oh, I'm not disputing she's at risk. But I can hardly go waltzing off for a place-of-safety order without something definite.'

'If we could at least get her in for a medical examination.'

'Again, only if we can find something more than just suspicions about the father.'

'Not just suspicions, damn it, every time he goes marauding around the park and . . .'

'Not enough,' Janet insisted. Then, pointing at Taff, she asked: 'What's this little Susan look like? Thin and weedy by any chance?'

The Welshman eyed her, then gave a slow nod, aware of her drift. 'Underweight for her age, if that's what you mean. Yes definitely. Likely physical neglect, no doubt of it.'

The social worker was nodding, satisfied with the contrivance. 'I'll have a word with the health visitor – maybe go in on a joint visit. That should be sufficient to apply for an order so as to get her into the hospital for the medical. But be warned, after Cleveland we're only getting orders for one week, That'll give only the seven days to get our act together for a full Care hearing in court.'

'Good evening, sir. Janet Heanley, Social Services.'

'Yes, Miss Heanley, do come in. Place-of-safety order, is it?' As the magistrate living nearest to the courts and council offices, Harry Palton got frequent hurried visits for the signing of warrants and orders. 'Charge a fiver for each of these, I'd be a rich man by now. Fancy a sherry while we go over the details?'

'Oh, thank you very much.' She stepped into the pleasant Regency town house, rich with the antiquities and books of the retired academic.

'Suspected physical neglect,' she explained, laying the paper out for him on a tooled-leather table beside the drinks cabinet, 'following my home visit earlier with the health visitor. A girl child of three.'

'Oh dear.' Harry Palton handed her the sherry along

with the Bible for her to swear the oath before asking her about the symptoms of neglect.

'Signs that she's underweight, sir. Failing to thrive.'

'And?' He leaned forward in search of other reasons on the order. 'Why the emergency? Why not wait till tomorrow in court?' Then, glancing at the social worker: 'Underweight on its own sounds a bit, er, slender, if you'll forgive my saying so.'

'Of course, yes, it does.' Janet nodded in agreement. 'Difficult, you see, to establish other symptoms until we can get her in for examination by the pædiatrician.'

'Indeed.' Palton was still staring at the papers, avoiding her gaze. 'The parents uncooperative, I take it?'

'Very.' Janet had in fact found the mother's response somewhat ambivalent. At first recognizing the health visitor, she had accepted their visit as routine and, indeed, had seemed prepared to bring Susan in to the hospital there and then for examination. But then the husband had burst in from listening in the next room; and, accepting his objections, the wife had promptly switched to resentment and hostility. 'But then, we hardly expected cooperation, given the background.'

'Oh? A known problem family?' Palton glanced at the name and address on the order. 'Snow? Gracious, not *the* Snow?'

'Yes, sir.'

'Ah.' The magistrate's frown registered his abrupt shift in priorities. It was one thing to exercise a check on over-eager social workers, but as for dealing with a local menace like Leonard Snow . . . 'A medical examination – yes.' He rubbed at his goatee beard. 'Yes, I can see the merits in that. Thin, underweight – yes, feasible grounds for suspicion, I dare say.' No need, he decided, even to check by telephone with the clerk. His pen was already out, his signature, date, time and place of signing already being entered on the order. 'Seven days then, Miss Heanley. Good luck.'

'Good evening, Mrs Snow, sorry to have to disturb you again but . . .'

'Go away!'

'I'm very sorry, madam, but I have to ask you to . . .'

'I'm not listening to you!' Sharon Snow would have shut the door, but the social worker already had a foot forward against the jamb to prevent her.

'Mrs Snow, I have a place-of-safety order for Susan. I'm sorry, but you have no choice in this now.'

'Wh-what you *mean*!' The mother ceased pushing at the door, her voice choking in alarm. She had heard but had not fully understood the implication earlier when this woman had referred to an order. Now, seeing her return, this time with a policeman, the fear clamped like a fist inside her chest. 'Susan's in bed!'

'If you'd just pack her a few things – a couple of changes of clothing, her toilet things, hairbrush and so on . . .'

'You can't! You can't take her away!'

'Purely for a medical examination, as I explained earlier . . .' Janet broke off as the mother was thrust to one side to be replaced by her husband, his eyes hard and menacing, his jaw grinding in agitation.

'Can't you people take no for an answer?' Then, catching sight of the detective-inspector standing in the shadows to one side, he pointed in rising fury. 'So that's it! Ain't enough forever banging me up on false rotten charges! Now you've got to get at the kid!'

'Mr Snow, if you'd allowed your wife to bring Susan to the hospital for a check-up, this order would not have been necessary.'

'Yeah! Check up for *what*? Making out I'd do things to my own blessed child now? Christ, you people! Your minds!'

Got you, Taff thought, watching in silence. So much for that superior arrogance now. Got you raging and scared if not on the run. Yet there was no satisfaction in it for the detective; only the revulsion he would feel at squeezing an abscess.

'The order's effective for one week, Mr Snow,' he remarked, stepping forward, 'at the end of which time, if necessary, the local authority may apply to a juvenile bench for a full Care order.'

'Where'd you reckon to take her?' the mother intervened, pushing forward again.

'The hospital, Mrs Snow. She'll be in the children's ward. Plenty of company and constant supervision. No need to worry.'

'No need!' the man snapped. 'You come here like Gestapo to snatch our kiddie away, and we've no need to worry!'

'Mr Snow,' Taff remarked formally, 'if you insist on prolonging this, that's down to you. But I have to tell you, this order carries the full force of a warrant. Unless you want to avoid a scene, which could upset the child more than she has to be, I suggest you calm yourself and leave your wife to fetch her down.'

Taff Roberts could see the fury burning fierce and deep in the narrowed eyes. Yet after a moment, he stepped back as his wife again pushed forward.

'You wanted me to bring her along down the hospital,' she called in her thin, bleating voice. 'All right then, I'll let the doc see her, but with me along with her.'

Janet's hesitation was only brief. The option was open to her as a compromise alternative to serving the order. Yet such a concession could work to their disadvantage in subsequent care proceedings. Moreover, to allow one parent along meant allowing the other as well, which certainly wouldn't do in this instance.

'Sorry, Mrs Snow, too late for that now. If you'd kindly

go and get Susan and her things. No need to get her dressed. Just wrap a coat over her night things; then we'll pop her straight back into bed as soon as we get her to the ward.'

In the event, the child took it badly: weeping in response to the mother's tears, doubtless also catching the aura of the father's intense rage. A child's attachment, Janet reflected ruefully, is no respecter of good or bad parenting. She murmured reassurances to the little girl all the way to the hospital but with scant success.

Taff Roberts went up with them to the ward, holding the endless swing doors in the endless corridors. Then they sat for a while by the bed while the ward sister fetched the hapless child a drink of hot chocolate and a biscuit – both duly rejected.

For a while, detective and social worker continued to stand nearby in the darkened ward after the sister had attempted to settle the child down, listening to the bewildered sobs, hating what had to be done. 'Ironic, I suppose,' murmured Taff as they finally turned way. 'Let's hope to God it turns out we're wrong.'

To Dr Anita Wilson, consultant pædiatrician at Marlbury General Hospital, specializing in child ailments had always seemed the only worthwhile form of medicine. Her love of children, after all, gave her the sensitivity crucial for reliable insights and diagnosis. Yet throughout the long years of study and specialization, the dimension of child abuse had remained alien and abhorrent to her. To combat the assaults of disease in her young patients was one thing: but to combat the warped assaults of adults was both unforeseen and repellent. The diseases of microbes and genes were impersonal, responding to drugs, radio-therapy and surgery; but the trauma of abuse was infinitely more complex, the damage less physical than psychological, the invasive organism a sly and defective adult immune to conventional methods of treatment.

Were it not for the devotion driving Anita Wilson, she would have happily abdicated on abuse cases and referred them elsewhere. Instead, with the rush of awareness and publicity in the mid-1980s, she followed her conscience, read it up as widely as possible, attended courses and seminars, and strove to subdue her abhorrence. That she succeeded was due not to zealotry for the cause but to love of those submitted to her care.

Whereas the likes of *Child-Watch* ventilated the issue and forced it into the public domain, the Cleveland furore did little to help Dr Wilson. A studious and retiring woman by nature, Anita had a horror of publicity equalled only by her unease at giving evidence in court. While adept at diagnosis and at one with the secrets of the consulting-room, she disliked the clinical detachment of forensic reports and quailed before legal counsel. But so be it. Abuse could no more be denied than diphtheria. And if the remedy lay through the courts rather than medical therapy, Anita would not shrink from the challenge. Whereas her police-surgeon colleague, Dr Shanks, might be struck all but silent by the Cleveland jitters, courtroom trauma was already endemic to Dr Wilson and, as such, not going to be allowed to undermine either her determination or her attack.

'This is Susan, Doctor – not the happiest of our young patients this morning.'

'So I see. Hello, Susan. I like your Teddy. What's his name?'

No reply, the child biting her lip as she stared tearfully at the pretty lady in jeans and sweater seated beside her in the room which, pasted all over with Muppet pictures, resembled a playroom.

'Talking of names, Sister, there's one missing here.'

The consultant pointed to the empty space at the top of the Social Services referral form. 'No surname?'

'Miss Heanley thought it best, Doctor, prior to your examination.'

Anita sighed, fearing that the ploy signalled something even nastier than usual in the woodshed. Nor did the cause of referral, *Failure to Thrive*, ease her misgivings. Whereas little Susan lacked the overfed plumpness of so many three-year-olds, she was not exactly the skinniest of waifs to be brought drooping and snuffling into the consulting-room.

'Well, being as it's Miss Heanley, I'll trust her motives and play along for now.'

She turned, leaning forward to address the somewhat threadbare teddy-bear. 'And what's your name?' Then, following a mumble from the child: 'Speak up, Teds, I didn't hear.'

'Leonard.'

'Leonard Teddy.' Anita wrote the name on a handy prescription pad. 'And why are you bringing Leonard to the hospital, Susan? Has he been ill?' Silence. 'Leonard, are you ill?'

'Yes.' The answer, although whispered, came in a whining little growl. 'Very.'

'Very ill, Leonard? Oh dear, what's wrong?'

'Want to go home.'

'Ah.' Anita glanced to the lower section of the referral form and noted that, as expected, Susan was in on a seven-day safety order. 'But, Leonard, one of the best places to cure illness is here in hospital.'

This brought a tiny growl which the doctor ignored, instead indicating for the child to remove the bear's tatty jacket. 'Let's have a look at you anyway, Leonard. Then we can have a look at your mistress as well to see if she's suffering from the same illness.'

The pretence, known in the trade as Circular Questioning, proved as effective as usual, the examinations proceeding in tandem: Teddy weighed, then mistress; Teddy's ears, eyes and throat, then mistress's; Teddy's tummy and bottom, then mistress's. In only one respect did the two examinations differ, namely that the child remained silent about herself, the necessary answers about her having to be elicited in gruff whispers from Teddy.

'All right, Sister,' the pædiatrician remarked, sitting back in relief as they concluded this rather laboured process, 'no problems: Leonard and mistress are both being properly fed and cared for, no signs of illness, parasites, neglect or abuse of *any* kind. Hooray. So very well, now we can fill in the missing surnames: Leonard and Susan?'

'Snow.'

'A normal, healthy, unabused three-year-old with only the one problem: very homesick.' Taff Roberts gave his landlady a rueful grin in irony and relief. 'Now what?'

Anne Cole eyed her lodger in concern. For all his attempted casualness, she could sense he was very strung up over the child's fate. As a policeman's wife herself, she had learned how vulnerable they could become. No better example, indeed, than David's predecessor, Les Hargreaves, the man's inner tensions driving him to that grim recourse, all too common among policemen, of drunkenly knocking his wife around. Unforgivable, of course, for all that the psychiatrists might rationalize it as a brutalizing consequence of their sickly job.

'Will it harm you with the Force, David?' Then, when he shrugged in indifference: 'What about Superintendent Leason? Does he know?'

'He may put two and two together, but I'd doubt it. Too busy fussing about overtime levels.'

'Well, if the child's homesick and no signs of harm on her, you'd best get her back to her mother and have done.'

'Oh, Susy's gone back home already. Taken back by the social worker, full of forced smiles and platitudes about safety-first and so on. Tearful reunion with Mum and virulent earful from wronged Mr Snow.'

'Well, then?'

'Well, then, what do we do now to protect her?'

'That?' Anne shook her head at him. 'Nothing, David. You've done your best. No one can expect more.'

Fifteen hours later, shortly after ten the next morning, two months after the assault on Vicky Bates, a ten-year-old girl was found sobbing in deep shock in an area of lightly wooded common land to the west of Marlbury. The girl's skirt and white socks were heavily stained with blood. The ambulance team called by the police to take her to hospital radioed in that she appeared to be haemorrhaging from a vaginal injury and to stand by for an emergency transfusion.

Chapter Nine

Taff Roberts hit the throttle like a demon, lights and siren full on as he headed for the Box Common estate. Beside him, Policewoman Hobbs braced back in her seat, awed by her chief's frenzy. Like poor old DI Hargreaves before him, she concluded, Mr Roberts was letting it get on top of him.

She was only partially right, since Taff's primary emotion was one of guilt. For he could see it now, clear and sharp, how it had ensued with the sureness of destiny: the monster in Snow, goaded by the forced removal of Susy to an extreme of manic defiance, raging out like a tiger in search of vengeance until chancing to find the lone child . . .

'Check for news from the hospital.'

'Jacquie's there, sir. She'll radio the moment there's anything.'

The WPC flinched involuntarily as a delivery van lurched against the kerb while swerving aside to let them pass.

'Sorry, Chief, but what's the rush?'

The detective made no answer but after a while gave a curt, angry shrug and slowed down. Val Hobbs reached out to switch off the siren, but he grunted to leave it blaring.

'No point in discretion, okay. We want everyone to know. Get 'em stirred up, get a lynch mob on the march, okay. Scare the shit out of the evil bastard.'

Val eyed him in concern. Normally so subdued and moderate; yet now his Welsh blood well and truly up. It would just need one taunt or abrupt word from Snow and they'd be embroiled in the whole dreary rigmarole of alleged police assault versus counter-claims of resisting arrest.

In the event, the nearest recourse to violence came from Sharon Snow. Still deeply distressed over the removal of young Susy, she reacted with instant bitterness to the return of the police, yelling incoherently from an upstairs window until her husband answered the front door. He was dressed in his usual turtle-necked sweater and slacks, his eyes cold and defiant as he stared at the two police officers.

'Mr Snow,' Taff asked, his voice tight in his throat, 'where have you been between six o'clock last night and ten this morning?'

'Been? Here, of course. Why?'

'The whole time?'

'Sure. Ask her.' He glanced up to where his wife was scowling down from the window above. 'Right, innit, Sharon? Ain't been out once, not since they brought Susy back home to us.'

'No!' She gestured in renewed fury at the two police. 'So get off and leave us be!'

Taff gave a curt nod, then resumed to the husband. 'Leonard Snow, I have reason to believe you are lying and I am arresting you on suspicion of committing a violent offence against a child.'

'You bastard!'

'You have a right to remain silent, but I must caution you that anything you do say may be written down and used in evidence against you.' He gestured the man down the path. 'Into the car.'

He looked up towards the wife, only to dodge sharply aside as she spat at him, then flung an ashtray in hopeless defiance.

'I understand how you feel, Mrs Snow, but Constable Hobbs has a search warrant so I suggest you cooperate.'

'Very wide on the time scale,' Snow commented as they got into the car. 'Sixteen hours. Don't you even know when this so-called violence was supposed to have happened?'

'Not yet,' Taff replied, his voice deceptively mild. 'Nor do we yet know the victim's full identity – nor, for that matter, whether she's going to live.'

'What kept you, Anita?'

'I had a special clinic out at Forley – got here as quickly as I could.'

The pædiatrician pulled on her face-mask while a nurse helped with her gown. Then, pulling on surgical gloves, she followed the casualty houseman into theatre.

'Why is she anæsthetized?'

'Frankly, there didn't seem much point waiting any longer – hysterical sobbing, incoherent – also inclined to thrash about when we tried to get the plasma drip into her.'

'All right, Prakash, fair enough.' She moved to where a nurse was mopping at the bleeding. 'Is someone on the way from Gynæ?'

'Ken Flint.'

'Good. And the police surgeon?'

'They're paging him on a domiciliary.'

'What about Photography?'

'For God's sake why? We don't run a cabaret down here.'

Anita eyed the Indian houseman as she moved across to the telephone, glad that her mask hid her irritation. Doubtless his offensive manner reflected his distress for the child, but it did nothing to help things along.

'Prakash, like it or not, this one's top forensic. Police inquiries *and* court reports.'

She got through to Photography, asked them to rush

107

someone down pronto, then moved back to the unconscious child just as transfusion arrived with the blood match. She noticed the ugly inflammation on either side of the victim's face where the assailant's hand had gripped to stifle her screams. Fortunate at least that her neck hadn't gone.

'I'll need to take a throat swab,' she told the nurse, then swung round on the casualty officer as he again exclaimed in irritation. A human enough response, of course, what with the helpless child lying there assaulted and bleeding; but this was a time for professionalism, not emotion.

'You're going to have to do out a report as well,' she warned him. 'Time, staff present, observations, plasma, anæsthetics, reasons, the lot.'

'For God's sake!'

'The more comprehensive,' the consultant persisted, 'the less likely you are to be called as a witness in court.'

'God forbid.'

'Only if you do it well, Prakash.'

'Labels?'

'One, sir, yes.' Jacquie Crane pulled a face as she indicated the name tag on a grubby anorak. 'Would you believe Patrick Smith?'

'Hm. Brother?'

'We've traced a Patrick Smith at Newton Primary.'

'And?'

'His mother gave the anorak for a school jumble.'

'Wonderful. No calls from anxious parents? It's nearly an hour since she was found.' He turned with a flourish as, seemingly on cue, the telephone bleeped beside him. 'Indecency.'

'Radio message from the search squad on the common, sir. They found a Labrador dog trailing its lead. Address on the collar is 15 Hale Green. It's beside the common, so the sergeant's gone along to check.'

It paid off. Within ten minutes, DI Roberts was heading for the hospital to hear it direct from the shattered mother, a blonde, portly woman with traces of a Dutch accent.

'We've told her, Mr Inspector, time and again we've told her: stay out in the open, don't run William in among the trees. But, well, I suppose if he got after a rabbit and . . . I mean, you know, a big dog like that, we always thought . . . and devoted to her, you see . . . bought as a puppy for her eighth birthday and . . . I mean, one yell from her and he'd be there to, you know, protect her. Then of course she always has her, whatsit, her shrieker thing . . . Her father got it for her in the States, you see. It makes a noise like a banshee . . . I know, I know, I know, I can see now how we were wrong – knowing that man had been about and, you know, doing those – those things. But to keep a lively girl like Selina cooped up like a convict when the common is right there beside our street and with a big dog like William to – to . . . Anyway, we thought he was in prison!'

'Ah.' DI Roberts wagged his head, his face a mask to any hint of judgement or reproach. Punishment enough to suffer the consequences. Moreover, he could find some sympathy over it: living beside open country, after all, their child bursting to go out and race around with her dog; they gave her strict instructions and a shrieker, and they let her run. Run straight into the jaws of the tiger!

'Why were we wrong, that's what I'm asking? Why wasn't he still locked away like we thought?'

'Perhaps you missed it in the local paper, Mrs Binks. The court released him beginning of last month.'

'Why? They had no right!'

He had the impression she was talking the way people often do in shock, their minds fastening on to things peripheral rather than on to the main focus of anxiety: the dog, the shrieker, the villain; anything but the fate of her darling lively girl.

'Oh, the court had the right, madam. And I'll tell you for why: because the parents of his last victim refused to let their little girl give evidence against him in court.'

'Sorry, Mr Inspector, I don't understand.'

'They said she'd suffered enough,' he continued bluntly. 'And as a result, your Selina's lying in there under intensive care.'

Denis Lisle found that his usual parking area in the police compound had been coned off so that he had to spend time finding an alternative space along by the council offices. It proved portentous, for his reception at the police station was far from cordial – as if, in some obscure way, he was being held responsible for his client's latest actions, real or alleged. Perhaps, he reflected ruefully, there was an element of truth in that – except that, given Leonard Snow's legal skills, his lawyer was largely incidental to his recurring liberty.

In any event, Lisle was increasingly unhappy about representing him. That new young partner with the firm, Jim Morton, had been mouthing on about experience in criminal work; so fine, he could take on the town's most notorious menace and give old Denny the break he deserved.

'Morning, Mr Lisle, seems like only yesterday you were applying to Judge Wallace for Mr Snow's release on bail, now here he is back inside again.'

The DI made no attempt to keep the irony from his tone before leading the solicitor along towards the interview room. 'Your man's singing a very different tune this time – hardly surprising in view of the circumstances.'

'Which are?'

The DI paused briefly, his hand on the doorknob as he

eyed the solicitor. 'Serious, sir. Could turn out extremely serious. In any event, a major change from his usual game.' Also, he thought to himself as he opened the door, quite possibly a change in the rules.

There was certainly a change in Snow's manner, the usual arrogance noticeably absent, replaced instead with a subdued watchfulness. The beast cornered and at bay, Lisle reflected, as he moved to his usual seat after exchanging a curt nod with his client.

'Right then, Mr Snow,' the DI began after he had switched on the tape and recorded the time and circumstances, 'having now been able to identify the victim, we're in a position to be more specific about times.'

'How is she?' The question came in a low, seemingly compulsive tone, taking both lawyer and detective by surprise.

'Pardon?'

'You told me – in the car, you said you didn't know if she was going to live. If you're set to try and stitch me with a serious crime, I want to know *how* serious.'

Taff Roberts hesitated, reluctant to yield possible bluff material. Yet he could hardly pretend the child was dead when she wasn't.

'Selina Binks is in intensive care which, as I'm sure I don't need to tell you, means her life is in the balance.' Then, more for the benefit of the lawyer than his client, he added: 'She's hæmorrhaging from severe vaginal injuries.'

Taff registered the impact on the lawyer – the jerk almost as though from an electric shock – then resumed to the sallow-faced individual whom all his CID instincts and experience told him was responsible. 'Suppose you start by telling us your exact movements from the time you woke up this morning.'

'Dash it, Jeremy, the man's got to be stopped!'

Jenny had heard the news report on the car radio while

111

fetching her father-in-law from the station. *Child found seriously assaulted on Thicket Common . . . now in hospital in intensive care . . . local man being held for questioning . . . AGAIN!*

'Distressing for you, of course, Jennifer dear,' Judge Harris intervened in that dry, definitive tone which so unfailingly needled her. 'But for the life of me, I don't see how you can expect Jeremy to stop him. Short, that is, of taking a knife to the evil so-and-so's testicles.'

Jeremy allowed a half-grin but was careful to avoid taking sides in a contest which he knew would end badly. It was galling enough for the branch prosecutor that he had had to hear of this latest assault from his wife. For once the law-and-order grapevine had failed and he would have to await the details until DI Roberts came to see him next morning to discuss the charges . . . which, by the sound of what Jenny and his father had picked up from the radio report, could turn out a lot tougher than Snow's usual . . . assuming, of course, that Snow was indeed the man in police custody.

It was a dread which secretly haunted the prosecutor, the fear that Marlbury's recurring child assaults could actually attract other sex offenders from elsewhere, opportunists confident in the knowledge that police suspicions would focus on the known local abuser. So far, thanks to Snow's routine of admitting contact with the victims but denying the actual abuse, this had never occurred. Yet the possibility persisted.

'Jeremy has specific guidelines defining both his role as prosecutor and the criteria for the charges he brings,' Judge Harris went on. 'Likewise, his independence, not only from the police but also from the conduct of their investigations, is enshrined in the CPS code. Hang it, my dear, one of the prime reasons the service came into being was to divorce investigations from the judicial process.'

112

'Ah yes,' she retorted, 'just as you'd have him divorce all emotion and humanity from it as well. Odd, isn't it, Judge – ' she only called him that *in extremis* – 'how the criminal courts are largely to do with sorting out *people*, yet he's not supposed to care or – or feel.'

She turned to her husband, flushed and close to tears as she moved to escape to the kitchen. 'You stick to your precious guidelines, Jeremy, and leave Snow to his fun.'

'The fair sex,' Judge Harris murmured teasingly to ease embarrassment as the kitchen door banged shut. 'Curious how we're letting so many of 'em into the profession these days.'

'Good evening, madam, WPC Crane, Marlbury CID. Sorry to trouble you but we're making inquiries about a violent incident which occurred between nine and ten this morning – yes, the one on the radio – wonder if by any chance you happen to recognize this child in the photograph or else saw a child out with a black Labrador dog between nine and ten a.m. in the vicinity of Thicket Common. No? Well, should you later recollect anything or hear of anyone who might be able to help, be obliged if you could contact the incident team on this number. Thank you, madam.'

Jacquie Crane was a well-built, sporty young woman with an open, self-confident manner well suited to house-to-house inquiries like this. Whatever she might have lacked in imagination, she made up in pluck and staying-power and as such, unlike her colleague Val Hobbs, she was less sensitive about any antagonism from the public. Thick-skinned by some estimates, yet that was a positive asset when tackling a run-down neighbourhood like the Box Common estate.

Unlike Val, she heartily approved of such tactics as the DI's use of the car siren when arresting Snow, also the phone-call she had later overheard him make to the newsroom of the local radio. Show the flag and spread the word, why not! After all, if crime threatened to engulf the community, why not challenge people to help fight back? Police in isolation made no sense of the latest calls for community policing.

Optimist and extrovert, Jacquie generally enjoyed her work, even on Indecency. It helped to feel that, regardless of jeers and prejudice, their work mattered.

'Good evening, madam, WPC Crane, Marlbury CID . . .'

'Here, just the very person I want to see – save me making a trip down the station.' The woman who had answered her knock was wiry and vigorous, dressed in a T-shirt and jeans, her eyes bright with excitement. 'Come on in, love. Inquiring about that poor kiddie up the Thicket Common, are you?'

'That's right, madam.'

'What time was it?'

'Between nine and ten this morning, Mrs – er . . .?'

'Darroch. Right, well I was up there, wasn't I, running my sister's little dog, Flash.' She nodded eagerly, eyes brighter than ever. 'And I saw that bastard Snow. Saw him sure as you're stood there. Saw him making off through the trees.'

'You know him then, Mrs Darroch?' Jacquie was trying to keep her voice even and calm. It could take hours and hours of dogged leg-work before hitting a response like this; but when it happened – oh wow! . . . 'Know this Mr Snow to recognize him in among trees like that?'

'Isn't a person on this estate doesn't know him, love.' She nodded in confirmation. 'It was him all right. He saw me and all – went dodging off to avoid me.'

There was something vaguely familiar about the woman. But it was only later, when taking down particulars, that the constable was able to place her as a part-time nursing sister whom she must have seen around at the hospital.

'We'll need you down the station later anyway, Mrs Darroch, to make a formal identification and also make a statement.'

'Fair enough. Got him arrested already, they said on the radio. Well, not to name him, of course, but no chance you'd be nicking anyone else for a filthy carry-on like that.'

Jacquie Crane was experienced enough to avoid any reply. It only needed a couple of prosecutions defeated in court due to indiscretions during inquiries and one very quickly learnt to give nothing away to anyone.

'We'll phone you soon as we've got the identification parade organized, all right?'

'I'll be ready, love. Anything to get that menace off the streets. Anything.'

The distress call was logged by the station sergeant at 10.08 that evening. He reached across to put out a radio call to the Box Common patrol, then thought better of it and instead phoned DI Roberts at his lodgings.

'Sorry to call you at this hour, sir, but it's pertinent to the Snow case. Contrary to procedure, of course, but some Hooray Henry just heaved a brick at the Snows' front door and I reckoned as you might prefer to respond to her call.'

'Dead right, Jack.'

Taff saw a group of three or four bikers along at the far end as he turned into the street and, further along, a tippler being walked by his dog. Otherwise, apart from a high-decibel throb from a teenage party four doors along, the street was quiet and deserted.

There were no lights visible in Snow's council semi, but Taff could see from the nearby street-light that one of the lower panels in the front-door was splintered by the impact of a half brick lying nearby. He eased the missile into a plastic bag while awaiting for Mrs Snow to answer his knock.

'Who is it?' She still hadn't put on a light, doing so and unchaining the door only after Taff had called out in identification. 'They smashed the door, look.'

'Yes.' He held up the plastic bag. 'With this. Did you hear them throw anything else?'

'Only abuse.'

Her choice of the word struck the DI as ironic, given her husband's habits. He pointed upstairs, hearing little Susan sobbing up in her bedroom.

'Upset the kiddie, did it, Mrs Snow?'

'She was upset before this. What you expect when you lot come after her dad!'

He could see that the young mother had been crying as well as the child – hardly surprising, in view of what she must have heard on the radio about her husband's latest exploits.

'Mind if I come in?'

'Why should you?'

'You telephoned for help, Mrs Snow.'

'I want protection, not a grilling.'

'I'll keep it strictly informal,' he said, crouching down to make some notes of the damage to the panel before moving into the house. He saw a light on in a backroom and, going through, saw it was the kitchen.

'You want to see to Susan first?'

'I told you, she's been crying on and off ever since you lot come and took her father. Only way she'll quieten now is to take her in my bed when I go up.' She turned to face him, her babyish features twisted in defiance. 'Now what's it you want? Here to put in more poison? That it?'

'No.' Yet it was a shrewd enough guess. Gullible and blindly loyal she might be, he thought, but not witless. 'We know he was up at Thicket Common this morning. We have a witness – a woman who was walking her dog

116

up there – she confirmed her identification at a line-up this evening.'

If it startled the woman, she hid it, her face turned away as she moved to tidy crockery from the drainer. 'Well, she's either a liar or she was imagining it, because he was here the whole time, like I said. The whole time, clear through from before they brought Susy home yesterday evening.' She swung round, fumbling a plate as she turned to face him. 'So there.'

He remained silent for a while, seeing how long she could hold his gaze before she again turned away. 'Loyalty's all very well, Sharon . . .'

'It's Mrs Snow, if you don't mind! Don't think you can come here and get familiar – not after all what you lot are doing to him!'

Another pause before he tried again. 'I respect your loyalty, of course. Mothered his child, making a go of it. But . . .'

'You think I could live with him all these years without *knowing*?' It burst from her constricted throat, so that she had to swallow before continuing. 'How could he do all what you keep saying and me not know, eh? You never ask yourself that?'

'Yes, Mrs Snow, often. You want to know the conclusion I came to? Not a very pleasant one but realistic in view of what we *know* about him.' He paused for a response then spelt it out for her. 'My conclusion is that you're part of his overall strategy – a cunning part, intended both as a long-term character witness and now also as an alibi witness. And . . .'

'Get out!' She gestured for him to leave and, in her nervousness, sent a cup smashing noisily to the floor. 'Poison was right!'

'You asked me,' he said, retreating from the kitchen.

'Not for that!'

'Can you,' he asked finally, pausing just outside the

broken front-door, 'can you tell me in all honesty that you feel safe leaving him alone in the house with that little girl of yours?'

The woman's strangled gasp and the desperate force with which she slammed the door, made the DI regret his brutality. Yet, God's blood, if she was prepared deliberately to false-alibi the bastard, so much for sympathy.

Chapter Ten

'It's very different this time around, Inspector. The savagery, the denial. I'm not disputing your decision to arrest him. Obviously right. But we must keep open the –'

'Sir, the denial follows on from the savagery.' Taff managed to keep his interruption mild, his irritation tempered by the fact that he had yet to inform the prosecutor of Mrs Darroch's evidence. But he resented it, none the less, when pussy-footing lawyers like Harris tried to tell him his job. 'More savage than usual, certainly. But, having injured the child so badly, he left himself no alternative but to hurry back home and tell his wife to alibi him.' Then, with a half grin, he went on to reveal how their door-to-door inquiries had located a positive witness to Snow's presence at Thicket Common and moreover that she had later confirmed identification in the line-up at the station.

To the detective's chagrin, the lawyer's caution persisted, Harris yielding only a brief grunt of satisfaction before asking how reliable a witness she was. 'After all, Inspector, given the intensity of feeling on that estate and the extent of personal animosity against Snow, we must be doubly cautious of –'

'Mrs Darroch is a nurse, sir, and mother of two kids at the local comprehensive. A perfectly respectable woman, hardly the sort to come on with a positive identification like that out of malice, if that's what you're suggesting.'

'It is, Inspector. However – ' Harris gestured in capitulation, sensing the DI's highly-charged mood – 'so long as you're satisfied with her veracity.'

'I have to admit, I've yet to interview her myself. So when I do, I'll make good and sure she's not swinging the lead.'

'Fine. How's the girl doing? Still in intensive care?'

'Officially, yes. But I understand the bleeding's stopped and she's no longer critical.'

'Thank heavens.'

'Still deeply shocked, however. Recognized her mum and dad but not much else as yet. Dr Wilson's still holding back with the investigative interview, but I've got WPC Hobbs standing by at the hospital in case.'

Harris nodded, glancing quickly through the Darroch verbals. 'Well, thanks to this, there's no hurry.'

'GBH and IA.' It was phrased more as a fact than a question, the detective barely waiting for the prosecutor's nod before moving to leave.

'It's all rather different this time, isn't it. Serious injury and denials.'

Denis Lisle paused, glancing in vain for some response in his client's yellowed, goat-like eyes. Try as he might, he could never penetrate the cold barrier of the man's stare – could plumb no hint of empathy, trust, respect, appeal – nothing to suggest that, after all these years the man saw him as anything other than an Establishment hack paid to go through the motions of representing his defence but never to be trusted.

'You'll doubtless be glad to hear the girl's not going to die – not unless some unforeseen complication sets in – so it won't be a murder charge.'

There was, he felt sure, just a hint of relaxation in the rigidity of the man – if only a slowing in the pace with which he chewed his gum.

'I didn't expect to see you in here today.'

'Oh? A serious charge like grievous bodily harm needs representation, even for the remand.' Lisle was damned if he was even going to broach the suggestion of a bail application. 'Why ever shouldn't I be here?'

'Reckoned you'd get shot of it. Hand it elsewhere.'

'After all these years, Mr Snow?'

In point of fact, shrewd-beggar Snow was right, the lawyer having indeed sought to dump the case on to young Jim Morton. No deal. Yes, by all means he would take on the rest of Lisle's court load. Stimulating challenge after all the conveyancing chores and contract drafting which the other partners were pushing at him. But as for plunging in with this one! 'Thank you, Denis, but no. For one thing, I'd have my prejudices to contend with – namely, a couple of bouncy, high-spirited and hence very vulnerable daughters; also a passionate belief in castration, chemical or actual, for kinky bastards like him. After all, it's one thing to defend a Careless Driving where you know your man's trying to lie his way out of it, or even to work the old Intent line on a shoplifter with a dozen previous. But frankly, to connive in getting that creep Snow off *yet again* – no, thanks!'

'It's likely to be his last. A dicky alibi; police and public all baying for blood; responsible adult witness for the Crown.'

'Denis old man, just tell me one thing: forget about all his other arrests, what about this one? Is he guilty?'

Lisle had paused then shrugged in rueful evasion. 'Not for us to judge but to defend,' he had murmured.

'For you, Denis, not for me.'

'Come across and sit down, Mrs Darroch.' Taff Roberts led the woman across the open CID area to his desk. 'Just a couple of points to check over on this statement you made to Constable Crane.'

He fetched her a chair, eyeing her as he tried to recall where he had met the chirpy, birdlike woman before.

'Neighbourhood Watch,' she said, reading his look, 'much good that's done us.'

Taff nodded, recalling the woman's keen, get-it-done approach – what some might have regarded as pushiness but which he for one had welcomed. Too often, house-wives were inclined to dither on; but this one had been quick-sharp on the uptake. If the Watch effort had indeed turned out less successful it was more because others on the estate had tried to use it to resolve petty grievances against neighbours rather than to prevent crime.

'Right, then,' she laughed, rubbing at her frizzy hair, 'what's the problem? If it's spelling, your Jacquie's the one who typed it out.'

'No, Mrs Darroch . . .'

'Dora, please,' she chipped in, pulling a face in self-deprecation.

'Okay, Dora. No, it's not spelling. In fact, there's nothing wrong with the statement itself so much as what could develop from it during examination in court. As things stand, it's likely to be a direct conflict of evidence: your identification versus the accused's denial that he was anywhere near the Thicket yesterday morning. So his defence counsel is likely to give you as rough a time as he can. Savvy?'

The woman nodded, biting her lip, her fizz of self-confidence suddenly on the wane.

'The more precise you can be about things at this stage, bearing in mind it'll be several months before it comes before a jury, the less vulnerable you'll be in the witness box.'

'For instance?'

'Well, what about the distance he was away from you?'

'Twenty yards,' she said with less hesitation than he'd have preferred. 'Cricket-pitch length. About the distance across this office floor.' Then, sensing his concern, she added: 'Look, a man like him, you notice.'

'Why?'

'Public enemy number one. Of course you notice him.'

'All right, Dora. But be warned, if you call him that in the box, you'll be inviting the accusation of prejudice.'

'Ah. Right.' She patted her lips, signalling discretion.

'Sufficient to say that you live on the same estate, you've seen him around and you recognized him that morning. Right, now then: his clothing. Did you notice what he was wearing?'

'Yeah – turtleneck, same as he had on in the line-up.'

Again the detective would have preferred less prompt assurance. 'Don't, Dora, don't mention the line-up or his counsel will use it to try and discredit your version. *He returned from this alleged violent assault, madam, and remained in the same clothing? Come now, I suggest the only time you saw him that day was during the identification parade.*'

She nodded, recognizing the trap. 'Well, when I said the same, all I meant was similar, that's all.'

'Then just leave it at turtleneck. And the rest? No coat? Chilly morning like yesterday?'

'Coat, yes. Well, jacket.'

'Colour?'

'Browny.'

'Checked, plain?'

'Checked.'

'Twenty yards away? Must have been extremely prominent checks.'

'Ah. Maybe it wasn't.' She gestured, the last of her assurance finally deserting her. 'Hard to be sure.'

Yes, Taff thought, and dead easy to discredit. 'Give it some thought, Dora. Better to say you don't recall than risk being tripped up on a point like that. Now then, the time: WPC Crane told me that you at first said ten o'clock but then switched to nine-thirty.'

'Yes, that.' She rubbed again at the frizzy hair. 'You see, I'd forgotten I got off work a bit early.'

'Oh?' To his deep regret, Taff was encountering increasing doubts. 'How come?'

'Things were quiet on the ward. I knew I had to walk Fanny's dog for her. Fanny's my sister. So my supervisor said I could pop off early.'

'How early?'

'About quarter to nine.'

'A quarter of an hour early?'

'About that.'

'And then?'

'Step by step?' She registered his nod, rubbing again at her hair. 'Ten minutes or so to walk home, another ten to change out of my uniform, wash and so on. A couple of minutes to go round to Fanny's to fetch Flash, twenty minutes to walk up to the Thicket.' She gestured, wagging her head. 'Nine-thirty.'

'Why the Thicket when Box Common is so much nearer?'

'I prefer the Thicket. So does Flash. More trees.'

It was a blasted pain, but he was finding her less and less easy to believe. It was all too glib and defensive, somehow like a kid caught out in a tale at school.

'This supervisor,' he asked, reaching for his pen. 'Name?'

'What? Oh, Wally Talbot. Why? Going to check with him?' Her tone was over-casual.

'This whole statement, Dora – you'll need to do out a fresh one with WPC Crane so as to include all these details. And, since that means mentioning your supervisor, that also means getting a witness statement in confirmation from him that you left early like you say. Also from your sister about the time.'

'And one from the dog, too?'

'This is no joking matter, Mrs Darroch.'

'I'm not laughing, Inspector.'

'Okay, then?'

'Yes, sure, why not?'

Why indeed, the DI thought. And the glaring, heart-breaking answer is because, Dora love, you are lying in your pretty, well-intentioned, Neighbourhood Watch teeth!

'Dr Wilson, she's been talking about it to her mother.'

'Well, jolly good, Sister, who better?'

'Except I know you prefer to try and be first.'

The pædiatrician smiled, struck by the alternative. 'You could hardly have barged in and told them to stop,' she said, moving towards the little side ward. She greeted the mother, then turned to Selina, relieved to see the transformation from the pale, corpselike form in theatre. The resilience of her young patients never failed to hearten her. Moreover, the child's recovery was a relief in view of the pressure to get on with the detailed interview.

'Feeling better for a good long sleep, Selina?' The face bruising had swelled and darkened now to a grotesque mask from which the child's eyes stared in alarm. 'Ready to tell us all about it, are you?'

'Doctor, Selina's told it all to me,' the mother put in quietly, 'so now, if I tell it to you, we can save her the upset of having to go through it all again.'

'I appreciate your feelings, Mrs Binks, but we need to go into a *lot* of detail.'

'Why? I don't understand?'

'For one thing, it's likely actually to help Selina if she can, so to speak, talk it all off her chest – purge some of the fears and embarrassment. Oddly enough, she's likely to do that more easily with experienced strangers than, well, with you.' Anita Wilson paused to nod encouragingly. 'Also there's the matter of identification.'

'The what?' The mother was frowning in ever deeper concern.

'There's a social worker and a policewoman outside ready with the video equipment.'

'Video?' Her alarm was of course perfectly reasonable, the consultant thought; it was the obligations of the law which were not. 'I don't understand.'

'It's not essential to tape the interview, Mrs Binks. On the other hand, if we make a fully comprehensive record this time, there's a good chance Selina won't have to be questioned about it any more – at least, not until the trial.'

'The trial,' the mother echoed. 'Can't – excuse me, but can't she just be left to get better first, poor love?'

Anita wagged her head, wishing she could agree. 'Except, the longer we delay, the less safe her recollections. After all, the trial could be several months away.'

The mother sighed, shaking her head. But then, recalling the detective's remark of the previous morning, she shrugged in acceptance and turned to her daughter. 'How about it, then, love? Remember how funny you were in that holiday video daddy shot in Holland last year?' Then, when her daughter remained silent and frowning: 'Mummy will be here with you.'

Albeit taking a back seat, the pædiatrician thought, moving to beckon the others into the side ward. 'It's like you'll have seen on television,' she explained to Selina, 'you know, when the cops are solving crimes. Except, this time, it'll be you there on the screen.'

Chapter Eleven

'And the girl?' Jenny asked.

'Selina? Well, I gather she identified Snow. She could have been more positive about it, apparently. But I suppose, having been so blind petrified by the man, she's bound to be a bit iffy.'

The sherry was being sipped upstairs this evening while Harris changed for a Masonic dinner.

'How is the poor little soul?'

'A lot better than might be, I gather. Physically, that is. What sort of scars the memory will leave is something else. But apparently Dr Wilson is reckoning on only a few days in hospital.'

'And what about this independent witness?'

'Ah.' Harris knotted his tie. 'She sounds quite promising, according to the police.'

'That's the Indecency inspector who you've got speaking to your lodge tonight, hm?'

Harris gave a rueful nod. He had first invited Roberts to talk several months back – well before even the Vicky Bates case. Now, coinciding with all the publicity and anger about Selina Binks, the choice seemed less than appropriate. Worse, with the savagery of this latest assault, he had sensed a disquieting zealotry in the detective's manner. Given their shared involvement in the case, any fiery Welsh indiscretions this evening would be doubly unfortunate. So much so that the prosecutor had earlier telephoned the station for a precautionary word with Superintendent Leason.

* * *

'So what can you as parents and respectable members of society do about law and order?' Taff paused to eye the ranks of well-dined faces before him. The strictures of the station super earlier on – 'stick to the old authoritarian line, Roberts: lashings of moral rectitude, puritanism and Jehovah à la Anderton' – had gone straight to Taff's Welsh Chapel heart. Yet it was a bitter irony that only hours before, the mendacious Mrs Dora Darroch had dragged him down into the sordid business of rule-bending.

'Most essentially, you could look to those tried old family values. Talk more to your kids, give them more of your time, set them a consistent example of behaviour. Also support their teachers and school discipline, likewise the courts and the efforts of the police – naturally!'

He paused to shoot them a teasing grin. 'I'm fully aware, gentlemen, that I'm speaking to the converted here. Not a womanizer or a tax-fiddler or an insider dealer present here tonight – much less any shoplifters or drunken drivers or, for that matter, child abusers.

'Statistically, however, if what we heard from Cleveland and elsewhere is accurate, the last of those is unlikely. If it *is* true that as many as one child in ten is abused, then that means a good few of you in this room were abused as kids and several *are* abusers. Now, now, don't let's start looking around at each other. After all, Masons aren't like that. Respectable people, Masons, who invite police officers to come and speak to their lodges. None the less, gentlemen, it's a startling statistic and one, I suggest, which we should ignore at our peril.'

And so on, fluent and challenging . . . while, beside him, Harris sat rigid and alert, his eyes scanning the reactions of his fellow Masons to this puritanical assault.

Yet, to the lawyer's relief, the final flavour was one of relaxed chuckles and applause as the DI rounded off his sermon with a wry twist.

'I forgot my prop,' he exclaimed, pulling out a large

black bushy beard and holding it up to his chin. 'I promised my chief I'd put this on and address you as God's Messenger in a Greater Manchester accent.'

'And thank you, Mr Roberts. One large brandy nightcap on its way.'

It was while Harris was at the bar ordering the drinks that Walter Talbot sidled up with a sly nudge and, when he turned to face the man, a conspiratorial wink. Whatever now? He was not a Mason with whom Jeremy Harris had ever had much contact in the past; something to do with hospital administration. A short, flushed, overweight fellow and, by the looks of him, none too sober.

'Like he just said, old boy, we should all of us do our bit towards law and order.'

'Sorry, er, Walter, not entirely with you.'

'That Snow bastard.'

'What about him?'

'Your copper was round my office this afternoon. Just a routine check, like.' Talbot's naturally red face made it hard to tell just how sober he really was; but, drunk or not, the man clearly believed they were all somehow in league.

'Our Dora,' he continued with yet another wink, 'she left work early yesterday morning, right? Left whenever she says, to do whatever she says – jogging or dogging, whatever. Just rest assured, Wally Talbot's not going to contradict her. Stand up and be counted, like your chap just said. Well, never fear, if it's going to nail that freaky bastard Snow, Wally Talbot is definitely, one hundred per cent your man. Rest assured on that, old boy.'

Rest Harris did not. Far from it. His lawyer's caution had curbed the impulse to march back to the DI there and then to demand an explanation. Instead he had returned with the brandies, drunk his own far too quickly and, after requesting a meeting with Roberts next day, had hurried off home where, although sorely tempted, he had refrained from sharing his anxieties with Jenny. The implications of conspiracy to perjury were, after all, far too serious for airing around, even with one's wife. So instead he had kept it to himself and duly spent a restless night fraught with indigestion and dread.

His team, swelled with even more agency lawyers than usual, seemed to be flapping over even the most straightforward of cases. By the time he had sent the last of them twittering off to court, he felt numbed and fuzzy, his mood anything but conciliatory as he called in the policeman.

'What about this Darroch witness, then?' he asked with more bluntness than intended as soon as they were alone.

'Sir?' Taff, who had expected at least some reference to his talk, braced himself for trouble.

'Yesterday morning, you promised to interview her yourself – to see if she's, in your phrase, swinging the lead.'

'Correct, sir.' They were both standing, the prosecutor beside the window, the policeman beside the ailing rubber-plant. 'Which I did.'

'And?' Then, when the copper gestured in evasion: 'What's her strength? More to the point, her veracity?'

Still Taff hesitated. Police investigations were not the province of the prosecutor, least of all at this early stage. Yet most clearly something had got the man stirred up – presumably that self-important burke of a hospital supervisor. Talbot's over-collaborative attitude when interviewed had alarmed the DI – and more so when he'd later encountered the man brimming with boozy nods and winks at the Masonic do.

'Her strength as a witness is excellent, sir. Articulate and positive; as credible as one could wish.'

'Then why involve her work supervisor?'

'Purely to verify her time of departure from the hospital. She told me she'd been on night-shift and had left fifteen minutes early because she'd arranged to walk her sister's dog. It seemed appropriate to check out that aspect with Mr Talbot.'

'And?'

Again the policeman resisted the impulse to remind Harris of his role in the system. 'And he verified it.' He opened the case file. 'If you wish to read his section-nine statement, you'll find it fully in order.'

'Oh, no doubt, no doubt. In so far as it goes.'

'Sir?'

'Talbot spoke to me last night, you see. End of the evening, well primed with drink and no doubt the stirring exhortations of your talk.'

'And?'

'And unquestionably he sees himself as being a party to some form of *conspiracy*.'

'Really, sir?' Taff, although reluctant to resort to it, could be as stolid as any copper at courtroom stonewalling.

'Yes, really. *She left whenever she says to do whatever she says*. His words. *Anything to nail that freaky bastard Snow*. Again his words.'

'Primed, as you say, sir, with drink.'

'But *in vino veritas*.'

'When interviewed, he gave me no indication of doubt or exaggeration or . . .'

'Perjury's the word.'

'Obliged, sir, thank you. No hint of perjury.' Taff, where absolutely essential, could lie as well as stonewall. He had known, clear as the sweat on Talbot's chubby face, that he was not only lying but had been primed to do so by a phone-call from Dora Darroch. The knowledge had disappointed him, of course; but solely in so far as it threatened the case against Leonard Snow. So their primary witness was dicey: too bad. At the very least, it would be several months before Dora's veracity was tested in court. If nothing else, hers would serve as ample *prima facie* evidence to ensure Snow's remand in custody if not ultimately his conviction. And meanwhile they'd have time on their side to see what else could be found.

'So what do you intend to do, Inspector?'

'Do, sir?'

'I'm telling you, the man as good as admitted to perjury. Which clearly suggests he's lying to shield Mrs Darroch's lies.' Then, persisting as the Welshman again held forward Talbot's statement: 'I don't care how bland his statement *or* hers. Putting it bluntly, at best this is *fudged* evidence. And that won't do.'

'Then it's just as well,' Taff retorted, collecting his case file, 'that poor little Selina gave us a positive ID of the bastard as well. Right, sir? Otherwise we might have had to release him.'

'The point at issue, Roberts, is just what you intend to do . . .' Harris's ultimatum was forestalled just then by the receptionist buzzing in apology to say she had the chief crown prosecutor on the line for him.

Berrington, so it turned out, was phoning to say he'd had the DPP's office on about this latest Snow case. Seemingly, MP Carlaw had decided to go further than his usual letter of protest by recruiting a full-scale lobby of Tory backbenchers.

'Not a warning, of course, Jeremy. Merely to, er, keep you abreast.'

Not surprisingly, when he rang off, Harris found the policeman had taken the case file and gone.

'They're stitching me up, Mr Lisle. That bitch Darroch's a phoney witness.'

The solicitor eyed his client dolefully across the prison interview room, watchful for clues in the man's demeanour. It was, of course, a predictable line for Snow to take. After all, since he was resorting to denials on the basis of an alibi supported by his wife, he was bound to claim that the Darroch woman was either lying or mistaken.

'I understand she's a respectable woman with no apparent reason to lie.'

'No reason?' Snow snorted in bitterness. 'Listen, she's a right little busybody, that one. Into everything: campaign for this, that and the other; running as a council candidate. Publicity-seeker, right? Anything to push herself into the limelight.'

Lisle gestured in deprecation, reluctant to take the point. 'Hardly valid grounds to try and discredit her evidence.'

'She had a go at my wife once and all,' Snow persisted. 'Got at her in front of a shop full of people.'

'Because of you? Your alleged, er, exploits?'

'Right. Setting herself up as the big defender of morals. Box Common's Ma Whitehouse.' Then, pointing in emphasis: 'Well, it's prejudice, innit.'

'Conceivably, yes. But hardly an issue counsel would risk opening up in court. To challenge her with prior prejudice, Mr Snow, would be to invite her to say *why* – which in turn would be to tell the jury about your background of suspected child abuse.'

Snow scowled, chewing vigorously for a while before conceding a reluctant nod. 'All right, but that don't alter the fact she's a phoney witness – put up to it by that poofter Roberts who'll have dictated every lying word of her statement.'

'That may be so, but –'

'It is so, my friend. And I'll thank you to make very sure Mr Mullins knows all about her when it comes to the trial. Soon trip that cocky bitch up in her lies, will our Mr Mullins.'

'We know it's him, Janet. You and me – we know it better than anyone.'

'Really?' The social worker shook her head, confused and perturbed. It had surprised her when, following the abbreviated formalities of the case conference on Selina Binks, the detective had come quietly up with the request for a cup of tea in her office. First that and then, the moment they were settled and alone, this implication that they shared some form of special knowledge regarding Snow's guilt.

It was ironic, too, since she had been at some pains to try and avoid confronting that issue. After all, her role as key worker on the case was solely to involve herself with the young victim, giving whatever rehabilitative help she could.

'I don't see how you work that out, Inspector.'

'Obvious, surely.' He sipped the tea, his eyes intense. 'You saw him too – when we went to get little Susy – saw his fury. No blame on you, of course. The responsibility for that whole ghastly cock-up – ' he gestured, his arms sweeping the air as though to embrace his guilt – 'for the trigger which unloosed his madness, was entirely mine. And, be sure, what Selina suffered because of that will damn well stay on my conscience.' Again he gestured, pre-empting her startled reply. 'No, no, that's my cross to bear alone. What I'm saying to you is – er . . .'

'That I also saw him provoked and raging that night – ' she nodded – 'and then the next evening when we took Susy back home – which you didn't see but which was every bit as fierce and vindictive.'

'And which,' he chimed in, 'was no more than eighteen hours before he was off to Thicket Common to find and savage Selina Binks!'

The social worker knew now why he had come requesting tea: to share if not to be absolved. 'You can't blame yourself, laddie. What you did was for the sake of little Susy. Supposing you'd been right and Dr Wilson had found evidence that he'd been assaulting his daughter . . .'

'If, if, if!' Once again the sweeping gesture. 'You could fill a book with *ifs* – the story of my life.'

'All right then, reproach yourself if it will help you feel better, why not! The vital point is that now you've *got* him. So Selina was a lamb sacrificed to catch the tiger. But now you've got him – got him on GBH, possibly on rape – the girl's evidence, Dr Wilson's evidence, *plus* an independent witness – what more do you want?'

Chapter Twelve

'Damn it, I can't condone it! I *can't!*' The shout burst
from Jeremy Harris in mid traffic jam, drawing a startled
glance from a driver in the next lane. Absurdly embarrassed, the prosecutor shut his window and switched on
the radio. The last time he could recall giving way to such
an outburst was over Jenny's mother and that had been
well over a year ago. Absurd and pathetic, letting a case
get on top of him like this. Time to take a rest – time to
delegate the load to Megan for a week or so and escape.
Great – except he could *not* for the fear of what he might
come back to. After all, but for that chance meeting with
Talbot, he would have accepted Roberts's word for it that
the Darroch evidence was *bona fide*. Perhaps best if he
hadn't known. But no, that would have meant proceeding
with the prosecution on a false premise with the high
probability of slipping up during the trial. In any event,
now he *did* know – was privy in advance to the conspiracy.
Now he was involved and vulnerable – and could *never*
condone it.

Whereas it was bad enough for the over-zealous detective to fudge up false evidence, it was unthinkable for the
branch crown prosecutor wilfully to condone that fudging.
Professional policeman was bad enough; but as for a
qualified lawyer in an esteemed position of public trust –
never! Harris had been sorely tempted that afternoon to
confide in Megan, to share his dilemma with a fellow
lawyer . . . except that, knowing Megan, she would
promptly have urged him to go with the conspiracy and
to hell with the ethics . . . which was all very well for an
Aussie but not, damn it, for a branch crown prosecutor.

Moreover, for all his need to share it, he knew it wouldn't be possible to tell Jenny. *Dash it, he's got to be stopped!* For sure, lawyer's wife or not, she would challenge his decision – his obligation – with all the force of a mother. Stuffy old lawyer, pompous and rigid, Daddy's boy . . . oh dear.

'Hello, Jenny love, how's your day been?' He could sense, even as he called out the greeting, that all was not well. 'Something up?'

'I'm not . . . well, it's probably nothing. Just mum-twitch, that's all.'

'To do with Carry?'

Jenny shrugged, avoiding his eyes, reaching to take his briefcase, then nodding as he remembered what evening it was.

'Brownies night.'

'That's right, but . . .'

'Not back yet?'

'It's only half an hour.'

'Who was bringing her?'

'No one. She and Harriet were walking back together.'

'*Walking?*' It was as though he heard his own voice shouting from a distance – as though he was standing apart watching his sudden frenzy. 'In God's name – you stupid woman!'

Taff Roberts took a gulp of whisky, aware of his landlady's disapproval but thankful she was sensitive enough not to voice it. It was seldom enough, after all, that he had a crisis serious enough to put him on the Scotch.

Talk things out man-to-man, that was what he needed, except that Harris wasn't the sort of bloke one could talk to. Nor was blooming Leason any better, a couple of career wimps together, playing it all strictly by the book, hiding their consciences behind the code, blinkered and inflexible.

And what the hell of a contrast to old Chiefie Walsh at the Yard. A man's man to the death; cunning and tough, blunt and ruthless, but with more native justice in his veins than a dozen of Harris and Leason rolled up together.

He sipped more Scotch, then tumbled the cat on its back, indifferent to the pain as it sank its teeth and claws passionately into his hand. Damn Harris. They'd stand more chance of begging old Denny Lisle to pull the defence than expect Harris to keep his nose out and his yappy little mouth shut. Perjury, Inspector! Grossly improper!

'David, will you leave that poor cat alone before it gets the taste of blood.'

Taff guffawed, dumping it on the floor. 'At least I've some blood for it to taste. Unlike a certain wet-rag lawyer.'

'Thank you, Mrs Haynes, sorry to have troubled you.' Harris banged down the telephone, his heart pounding, the blood pulsing in his temples and his ears. 'How *could* you!'

'Jeremy, stop it! Please!'

Yet he couldn't – couldn't swallow it back any more than he could believe she could be so callous and stupid and negligent.

'It's not as though you had anything else to do. Not as though you worked at a job or had commitments!'

'*Please.*' She was crying now but in humiliation more than anxiety.

'What about Harriet's mother?'

'What about her?'

'Does she know you're just – just letting a couple of ten-year-olds wander around . . .'

'Of course. Her suggestion, as it happens,' Then, scarlet-faced in retaliation: 'Twelve and eleven, they are, not ten-year-olds. Not babies. Another year or so and they'll be out baby-sitting!'

'Really! And how does that make them any less vulnerable and exposed to – to . . .?'

'To *what*? The monster's in prison, isn't he? That's what all this hysteria's about. That lunatic Snow.'

'Rubbish.' Yet he knew she was right. The neurosis, the phobia. Crucially right. But in unconsciously turning it back on to him, she had merely made it worse, goading him by implication with his own ineptitude to stop the man. 'Downright irresponsible!'

'Oh, so sorry, Mr Lawyer. Mr Judge's son!' Then, seeing him swing blindly away towards the door: 'Wait! Where are you going?'

'To search for them, of course. And meanwhile, you get on to the police.' He paused in the doorway to glare back at her, was drawing breath for a parting rebuke when he felt the touch on his hand and spun round in shock.

'Daddy, what's wrong?'

What's wrong? *What's wrong?* The bottom just fell out of my life, that's what! My daughter – my sweet, irreplaceable Carry-Caroline – was laid mutilated and defiled in my mind, that's what! For the duration of a hundred years which was actually a few minutes, for a thousand frenzied phone-calls which were in fact only two, for the exchange of a million cruel and irretrievable words yelled in seconds, that's what!

Caroline, sensing the extent of her father's stress, dodged aside and fled to her mother. 'Sorry, Mummy. We only went for a quick look at Harriet's pony, that's all.'

'What's that mad copper want, ranting on at me about intimate samples? What the hell's he up to now?'

Denis Lisle nodded, staring solemnly at his client and

secretly relishing the prisoner's state of panic. Earlier in the day, the lawyer had sat alone in front of a television set at the police station watching the video-taped interview with Selina Binks. It had been profoundly disturbing. Whereas the child's identification of Snow had been open to some dispute – largely because being shown his picture had produced more shock and rejection in her than a positive affirmation of identity – the visible distress of the victim had been deeply shocking. Her stammered description of the assault, its abrupt savagery and the paralysing horror with which she had been gripped, showed that even at the time of the recording, barely a day after the incident, she could recall and articulate only a jumbled impression of pain and terror . . . Confused, yes, and yet the impact on the defence solicitor had been, in a sense, the more shocking for that very lack of precision, hence leaving it to the observer's imagination to fill in the details as underscored by the horrific mutilation, bruising and shock.

Lisle would have liked to show that tape to Snow. He could yet do so on the pretext of reviewing it as a possible aid to the defence, ludicrous though that proposition clearly was, but in fact to show it to him as evidence of the intense misery resulting from such bestiality. Yet he would not do so, less because of any doubts of his client's guilt as because of his certainty that the man's arrogance and total lack of remorse would leave him with nothing but a sadistic relish from watching the tape.

'Yes, Mr Snow, Detective-Inspector Roberts showed me the authorization to collect a blood sample – fully in order, countersigned by his station superintendent. Assuming you consent, the prison doctor will collect it for dispatch, half to the forensic labs, the other half to us for independent grouping. Of course, under Section 62 of the Police and Criminal Evidence Act, you're fully entitled to refuse. But if you do so, the prosecution will be at liberty to comment on that refusal.'

'But why blood? Damn it, what are they after?'

'A saliva match, so I understand.' He pointed at Snow's mouth. 'Your habit of chewing gum.'

'Gum?' Snow's jaw promptly froze in alarm.

'That's correct. I understand the consultant in charge allowed the victim to be taken up to the Thicket to show the police where she was assaulted. Following a comprehensive search, a piece of, er, masticated chewing-gum was allegedly found in the immediate vicinity. Naturally, in view of your gum habit, they now require this blood sample for a possible saliva match.' He shook his head. 'Snow, I really don't see what you have to laugh about.'

Not that there was any humour in the sneer twisting the prisoner's lips. 'The sly bastard,' he grunted. Then, pointing in bitterness: 'I can tell you exactly where he got that bit of gum from and it wasn't no bloody Thicket.'

'Then where?'

'Police Transit. That time they took me and the family off to Wiltshire.'

'Ah.' Oddly enough, Lisle was weighing it less for veracity so much as its likely impact in cross-examination. *We know you accompanied the accused to Wiltshire after his release on bail, Inspector. You expect the jury to believe he chewed no gum on that occasion?'* 'Well that's certainly a useful explanation.'

'Useful! Christ sake, it's *true.'*

And, for once, Lisle was inclined to believe him. DI Roberts, after all, was no novice. He would know, from bitter past experience, the vulnerability of witness identifications, not least where prejudice could be implied, as seemed likely with the Darroch woman.

'Well then,' he said, wishing that he could in all conscience advise the opposite, 'you'd be wise to give them their sample and trust in Mr Mullins's undoubted skills in cross-examination.'

Taff closed the office door and stood stiffly beside it while the station superintendent sifted papers on his desk. Sure as hell, this was going to be the carpeting he had expected ever since his bitter meeting with the branch prosecutor. He had fully expected to hear from Harris the very next morning; but the subsequent silence of several days had convinced him the lawyer had instead decided to pull rank and complain at top level. Given that Taff was still trying to live down his transfer from the Met, in effect putting himself on probation with the Thames Valley force, this was doubly vexing. Whereas Leason was reasonable enough as station chiefs went, Taff reckoned he was unlikely to back a renegade Met DI who had taken it on himself, as Harris claimed, to fudge the evidence in what was going to be a major public trial.

True, there need be no question of any disciplinary action – not if he stuck to the line he'd taken with Harris. Yet Leason would know; he'd recognize it as a specious pretence and would duly add another adverse note to Taff's already tarnished service record.

'Your talk went down well with the Masons, I hear.'

'I hope so, sir.' Don't be misled by any diversionary tactics.

There was a longish pause as the super glanced through various papers on his desk.

'One or two worrying comments from Dr Shanks on your annual medical report. He refers to signs of stress and anxiety – also says you mentioned working excessive hours.'

'Hardly something I'd expect criticism for, sir. It's not as if I'd been whacking them in for overtime.'

'Concern, not criticism, Roberts. Taken in conjunction

with your, er, excess of authority over Snow's bail transport – know your enemy, all the flap over his little daughter and so on . . . No, no, hear me out. I'm not raising any of that in rebuke, merely as an extension of this concern expressed by Dr Shanks.'

Here it comes, Taff thought: *also as a symptom of this most disquieting report from the Branch Crown Prosecutor* . . .

But no. Instead, the chief's features pinched into a half-smile as he gestured for Taff to sit down.

'Wouldn't want you cracking up, Roberts. Indecency isn't the cushiest of numbers, least of all with an animal like Snow to deal with.'

'It's certainly a contrast to what I was doing up in the Smoke, sir.'

'Yes.' Pause, his eyes back on the report. 'How do you feel? You want to apply for a transfer? I could find you a place with Serious Crime.' Pause. 'No reflection on your handling of Indecency. Don't think that. Simply, well, shades of Les Hargreaves before you. Les kept it all inside, so to speak, and look what happened.'

Taff's knowledge of the Hargreaves trouble was limited largely to what he had heard from Annie Cole – booze and wife-bashing as a stress reaction to the job.

'Since it was Snow who saw Les off the pitch, sir, that gives me all the more cause to nail the bastard – quite apart from the plight of all those little girls.' He stood up. 'If it's okay with you, I'll stay with Indecency for as long as it takes to finish off what Les started.'

The chief nodded, closing Taff's personal file. A reprieve, thank God!

'And indeed, a probable end in sight for Snow, yes?' Briefly Taff considered mentioning the weakness of Dora Darroch's evidence, if only as a precaution. But then his chief pre-empted any reply with a typically feeble joke.

'Provided, of course, that you can make that piece of gum stick it together for you.'

The cell was small and featureless, the walls painted battleship grey like everything else in the punishment block. The one advantage was that, unlike other remand prisoners, Snow had the cell to himself, having applied under Section 43 of Prison Rules to be isolated for his own protection.

He had several books to read – volumes on historical military costumes, also books on law – brought in to him by Sharon. And it was the least cherished of these that he was at present engaged in tearing apart, crumpling each leaf into an ever-increasing pile on top of the iron-framed bed. The process involved careful calculation since, while he daren't risk overdoing the amount, the ploy needed a fair degree of credibility. In the event, he decided that three books, yielding several hundred crumpled pages, was ample; whereupon he turned to the bedding which he tore into strips to lay carefully on top of the paper. Finally, checking his watch, he moved to listen at the door of the cell for sound of the warders' shift change, due on the hour.

The moment he heard the familiar clang of the block's entrance door, he moved across, struck a match and applied it to the pages at the bottom. The flame caught, spreading with alarming hunger up through the pile. Hurriedly the prisoner moved to lie flat on the floor, his mouth close to the gap at the base of the heavy iron door. He listened to the whoosh of flame as it ate greedily into the tinder pile, felt the sudden draught of air sucking in under the door; and with it he experienced a sudden, exquisite rush of fear that the discipline officers, perverse and hostile towards him as they were, just might decide there wasn't that much of a hurry to respond to his cries for help.

* * *

'As we've both learned to our cost, Inspector, prosecutions under the Obscene Publications Act are notoriously fickle. Best hold off on this one.' There was, of course, no way Harris could avoid meeting Roberts on other court matters like this. 'Anything else to discuss?'

The DI gathered his case papers and stood up, eyeing the prosecutor with the stiff formality which had prevailed between them ever since Talbot had blabbed. 'Only, sir, to say I'm obliged for your discretion over the Snow case.'

'Ah.' So now it was in the open; now what had hung like an unspeakable disease between them ever since the Masonic evening was out. 'Just don't interpret it as a condonement, Roberts.'

The truth of it was that his impulsive decision to stay silent – to ignore it and hence to share in the perjury – had come as an extraordinary relief to Harris. That it had taken the panic over Caroline to make him breach the code now seemed almost irrelevant. For the relief ran far deeper than that acute moment of truth on Brownies night, representing in fact something of a liberation.

All his life, as far back as he could recall, Jeremy Harris had had it drummed into him: your integrity is your bond, boy . . . dedication to probity and the rule of law . . . personal conduct at all times scrupulously above reproach . . . stay on that road and it'll lead you clear up to the very top.

Well now, in that single wild moment, he had defied those rigid strictures, yet in doing so had unwittingly liberated himself from a cell he had only then realized existed.

Paradoxically, he felt neither guilt over breaching the code nor anxiety over the risk to his esteemed career. The prevailing sensation, even days after the fatal decision, was still one of release and elation. His only regret over the whole amazing business was his acute shame at the way he had behaved towards Jenny, ranting on and accusing her of negligence at the very time he should have remained calm and supportive; regret, too, that for so many years he had failed to side with her against his mentor Judge Harris. Stuffy, pompous, Daddy's-boy lawyer. Oh yes, he could see now that she was right, for all the coldly rational imperatives which had seemed to dictate that he conform to the role.

'I wouldn't dream of it, sir,' the policeman replied. 'In any event, condonement implies a degree of guilt, whereas I've no doubts about the ultimate justice of bringing Snow to book.'

'That end justifies the means, however corrupt?'

'Snow's end, yes.'

'And what if the assault was by some opportunist sex offender from outside and Snow is genuinely innocent?'

Taff was nodding, the possibility far from a new thought to him. 'Still no injustice, Mr Harris. Simply set it off against all those other assaults he's got away with.'

'It's a slippery slope, Roberts. Get away with it the once and – ' The lawyer shook his head, meeting the detective's level gaze. 'A fatal habit to slip into.'

'Agreed, sir.'

'The danger, don't you see, is of confusing, let's say, crusading zeal with arrogance and abuse of power.'

'Infamous,' Taff murmured ambiguously, moving to leave. Whereas he had no qualms about the perjury, it was a huge relief none the less if the prosecutor had indeed decided against rocking the boat. Less of a wimp than he'd seemed.

'You'd best hope,' Harris warned as Taff opened the door, 'that it doesn't turn out you've sown the wind only to reap the whirlwind.'

I examined Leonard Snow in the prison hospital where he had been taken as a precaution following a fire in his cell in the isolation wing. No burns sustained and, according to the prison doctor, Dr John Martin, injury limited to inflammation of the lungs and bronchi due to inhalation of noxious fumes. I put it to Snow that he had started the fire as a form of calculated protest, but he maintained the intention to take his own life. Asked why, he retorted that he was at the end of his tether and could take no more persecution. It is his contention that, ever since his initial conviction for indecently assaulting a nine-year-old child several years ago, he has been the target of a sustained vendetta by the authorities, principally by the police, he says, but with the ready collaboration of the courts and prison staff. It was the taunts of the latter, he claims, which had driven him to this suicide attempt. But he then went further, insisting that the police, abetted by his solicitor and Dr Martin, were now pressing him to give a blood sample. The intention, he vehemently insists, is to deceive him into the belief that he is a victim of AIDS syndrome. In short, whether genuine *or* ingeniously contrived, Leonard Snow exhibits the classic symptoms of paranoid psychosis, as manifested by persecution mania and obsessive delusions of conspiracy by the authorities.

P. J. Wilmot, Prison Psychiatrist.

'Come on, out with it: what strength Crown *v.* Snow?'

'Ah.' The lawyer's caution and the impulse to prevaricate were still there; only the resolve had changed. 'Very strong.'

'No kidding!' Megan plumped down in the chair opposite his desk, case files clasped to her athletic chest, eyebrows arched to cue his explanation. 'That good on the GBH?'

'That good,' he confirmed, his face a mask. 'A solid

independent witness; positive ID by the child; confirmation of sexual assault by the pædiatrician; *and* a piece of Snow's chewing-gum found at the scene of the crime.'

'Bingo!' Yet, disconcertingly, he noticed Megan's eyes failed to mirror her enthusiasm. Why? What did she know? What *could* she know? 'And it's all going to stand up in court?'

Harris heaved back in his chair with a rueful gesture. 'As usual, we're in the hands of the Constabulary for that. But – well . . .'

Her gaze, he noticed, was still searching and unsure. 'DI Davy Roberts, right?' Then, at his nod: 'Dedicated, cool, and, if his Masonic performance was anything to go by, Chapel straight – yes?' Pause. 'Jemmy, what's the matter?'

'*Nothing.*' Then, with more composure: 'Nothing at all.'

'Great.' She wasn't deceived. 'Then there's nothing to worry about. Snow's for the drop at last.'

PART THREE

Chapter Thirteen

Chiefie Walsh drew on his cigar, easing back in his chair with an elaborate belch. He was sublimely content, his mood fortified by the Scotch, red wine and rich food of their squad reunion dinner, also by the opulence of his well-paid retirement job with a firm of City bankers . . . that time in the life of an ex-Chief Super when all the dirt and the compromises have withered in the memory sufficient for myths to germinate and past cases to bloom into legend. And no one better to cultivate them with than his fresh-faced one-time protégé, Taff-the-lad Roberts, with whom he had shared his last and most spectacular few cases before retirement. *By Christ, lad, you remember the look on that DAC's prattish face when it all came out about the Cabinet cover-up* . . . Except that, for all the booze and the laughs and the after-dinner kissograms, young Taff was not relaxing the way he should. Not that he was countering the myths or denying them legend status. That would have been rank heresy. But he wasn't letting go in the way Chiefie Walsh had anticipated.

Of course Taff hadn't been silent. He'd ventilated at length about his transfer to the Thames Valley force and the legacy of suspicion he was still having to live down as an ex-Met officer; also, he had let go something of the angst of running Indecency in a town which had doubled in size in the last twenty years at grievous cost to its sense of community and social responsibility.

Yet there was more. Walsh knew it with the sensitivity of a father for the son he'd never had.

'Got a big one on the boil, have you?'

Taff gave a rueful nod, reaching for his glass. 'Listed for Wednesday at Reading before Judge Pile-Driver Wallace.'

'Leonard Arthur Snow, GBH and sexual on a child.'

'How the bloody hell did you know that?'

'Word gets around.' That wasn't strictly true since Walsh had been at some pains to find out. Unstretched by his security job, he took pleasure in running the occasional remote check on his protégé's activities. Snow's name had blinked up on the VDU screen with depressing regularity. 'I tell you straight, Taff, that's what would rile me most of all on Indecency – having to watch child-abusers like him screw the legal system even worse than their little victims.'

'This one's got a kid of his own,' Taff remarked abruptly. 'Little blonde kiddie of three.'

How could it fail to sicken those charged with its containment, Walsh thought. Not only sicken but warp and embitter. And Taff more than most, given how special kids were to him, in the way unmarried blokes could be who longed for parenthood. 'And you reckon she's . . . ?'

'At risk, yes,' the DI confirmed, 'eventually.'

'Unless you can nail him this time round, eh?'

'Right.' There was a crispness in Taff's retort totally at odds with the skinful of booze he'd put away throughout the evening. 'Right on.'

'Here, Taff, you're not playing silly buggers over this one, are you?' Then, when the Welshman offered no denial, instead reaching curtly out to refill his glass: 'What have you got on him, anyway?'

'Ten-year-old victim, for what *she's* worth.'

Walsh grunted, all too aware of the indifference which the judiciary showed to children's evidence. 'And?'

'An independent witness – who happens to be lying in her teeth but who just might hold up.'

'What about the medics?'

'An emotional pædiatrician likely to go over the top because she cares too much.'

'You and all, boyo,' Walsh chided. 'Anything else?'

'Yes,' Taff murmured casually, 'handy bit of forensic saliva matching on a piece of chewed gum.'

'Where'd you find that?' the ex-Chief Super snorted. 'Stuck up her gunga?'

'Leave it out, guv. It's genuine.'

'Oh, sure! Just like you're a genuine twat!' Then overriding the DI's protest: 'You never could lie to me, Taff lad, so don't try it now. But, by heck, you must bloody care about this one to pull a prattish stunt like that!' He snorted again. 'Chewing-gum, by Christ.'

'He's *got* to go down, guv'nor. He's bloody *got* to!'

It was a relief, none the less, to confess – to unburden to this gaunt, lantern-jawed giant who, for all his cynicism and foxy ways, for all his corner-cutting and dubious methods, ranked second only to his dad in Taff's calendar of saints.

'For the sake of little Susan and for countless other kids in and around Marlbury.' Then, pointing with the earnestness born of too much drink: 'I tell you, guv, this time I'm beginning to think he *wants* to go down.'

'Ha!'

'No, no, I honestly do think he's sick of the game. Not remorse. Not that. Never. Classic psychopath, if you ask me. But, I don't know, I just get this gut feeling that this time he's, like, throwing in the towel.'

'So big-hearted Taff's doing him the almighty favour of stitching him up with a bit of his own gum. By Christ, boy, you of all people!'

'Don't tell me *you* never did it, Foxy, because I know you did!'

'Except it's not me we're talking about but *you*.' He gave a wry snort. 'The one and only bastard who could have done that to me two years ago.'

153

'Done what?'

'Shamed me, boyo, that's what.' He snorted again. 'Shamed me into disobeying orders and following my lousy old conscience for the first time in all those years, that's what!' He belched again, only to swallow back the acid bile at the back of his throat. 'And now here's that same pious crusader for truth stitching up a noncy little wanker and no better than the rest of us.'

'Yeah.' Taff grinned drunkenly, suddenly no longer ashamed of his decision to plant the gum. 'Well, that's the legacy for you, guv'nor – the penalty of working two years on Indecency. Changed priorities. Call it corruption if you like. But it still feels like a crusade.'

'Where's Susy? You promised.'

'I know, Len, but she's still got that cold.'

The prisoner scowled at her, contemptuous that she couldn't even think up a more original lie. He sipped the WRVS tea, aware of the glances directed at them by the villain and his family at the next table. Pompous flipping bank robber; it was thanks to the likes of him he had to skulk away in the isolation wing. Well, sod you, mate, come the end of next week, Len Snow'll be a free man again, free to get on with living while you rot in this poxy hole!

The one doubt – the one and only worry – was Sharon and her reason for refusing to bring little Susy. Poisoned against him, perhaps, her mind poisoned by that nutter of a DI?

'Been to see you again, has he? That copper?'

'No, Len, I'd have said if he had.'

Well, tough. Roberts was going to pay for the one visit he had made. Harassment of the key defence witness: Mullins'd see he didn't get away with that!

'Leonard.' She was staring at him again, her baby face

twisted in a blend of uncertainty and pleading. 'Tell me you . . .'

'I did already. Every time you come, I tell you.'

'It's just that – stupid of me, I know – but, well . . .'

'It was that copper coming like that to whip Susy away on that order!' His hands were clenched, the jaws grinding like a mill. 'I just had to get away, right. Had to move out and run and – and get some air into me. Don't you see, Sharon, that's why I tried all that with the fire in my cell. Soon as I get tense and wound up, there's no way I can take being closed in.' He paused, reaching for her hand, but she jerked involuntarily back. 'I just had to get out that time.'

'All night?' she whispered. 'And then – then, coming back home all messed up?'

'You try running all night, Sharon, and see if you aren't messed up.' He managed to keep the impatience from his voice. It was galling to have to depend on the bleating idiot for once. Yet depend on her he did, no denying that. 'If you stop believing in me, Sharon love, that's the end. You know that, don't you. It's only 'cos you've stood by me all these years while they've been getting at me – that's the only thing's kept me going. Okay, this time that sod Roberts reckons he's got me stitched up and done for. But we mustn't let him get away with it, eh?'

He paused briefly to gauge her resolve, trying in vain to trap her evasive gaze. 'Tell you what, Sharon, get through with this lot and we'll move away, right? Get the hell away and start fresh.'

'But where, Len? You always said they'd – '

'The Falklands,' he interrupted her. 'That should be far enough.'

'You don't mean that.'

'I *do*. You know me. I'd never lie to you, Sharon.'

* * *

'Obliged to you for arming me with rather more than a cardboard sword this time, Inspector.' If there was an irony behind Counsel Prosser's remark, Taff could detect no hint of it. The irony, he reflected, lay in the fact that he and Harris both knew what she did not know: that, if not cardboard, it was certainly hollow. There was no way Miss Prosser could be told, nor much she could have done about it even if she did know. Yet the tired old maxim prevailed: always be sure and know the *true* strength of your case in advance. Which Counsel Prosser did not.

No doubt she had her own secret views about the validity of the chewing-gum, being no more naïve about such items than old Chiefie Walsh. Yet propriety if not delicacy forbade any direct challenge by her of a senior officer prepared to go on oath about its veracity. She might, during Taff's examination in chief, seek to anticipate Mullins's attack but nothing more. However, as for Dora Darroch . . .

'Inspector, this section-nine statement from the nursing supervisor, Talbot: singularly assiduous of you to collect that in advance.'

Taff shrugged, his glance shifting involuntarily to the branch prosecutor. 'Since Mr Mullins is bound to challenge the timing, it seemed prudent.'

'Granted.' Edwina Prosser was always cautious of detectives who got too smart in anticipation of defence counsel's tactics. 'The risk, of course, is that we signal doubts about the strength of Mrs Darroch's evidence.' She glanced towards the silent branch prosecutor. 'Is there a weakness?'

Pause, Harris making rather a business of searching out the woman's witness statement.

'There's no need for that,' Edwina remarked. 'I've read it through *ad nauseam*.' She switched her glance to Taff. 'Well, Inspector?'

'Something wrong with it, Miss Prosser?'

'Only that it's almost too good to be true.' She smiled thinly, reaching for her cigarettes. 'Rehearsed, one might even suspect.'

Taff shrugged in apology. 'One just might be right, ma'm, given how central she is to the Crown's case.'

Pause. This is it, Taff thought: this is where wimp Harris loses his bottle and screws up. But no, short of fidgeting excessively through the pages of Dora's statement, the man held firm.

'You, as it were, doctored it then, Mr Roberts?'

'Merely encouraged her to elaborate on what she'd originally said to WPC Crane, ma'm.'

'Whose name none the less remained on the statement as the interviewing officer.'

'I – er – ' Damn the woman for her sharpness. 'I explained to Mrs Darroch. She won't mention it.'

'No?' Edwina puffed smoke like an elegant dragon. 'Let's hope not. Samuel John Mullins can get very pushy when he smells a rat.' Then, topping Taff's reply: 'Conspiracy to amend a witness's evidence, Inspector, is *not* likely to impress the jury.'

Another pause, Taff squirming in the hot seat. Briefly the barrister glanced at Harris, who in turn glared at Taff but still remained silent.

'I need to know, that's all,' Edwina resumed, her tone softening slightly. It gave her no more pleasure to attack a well-intentioned, not to say dishy, detective-inspector than to start unpicking the police case. Yet for all the apparent muscle bulging the statements in her brief, the vibes were somehow wrong.

'Yeah, well . . .' Taff gestured in discomfort. 'I'll make sure and warn Mrs Darroch again on that point.'

'Let's hope it doesn't throw her confidence.'

Which, Edwina reflected as she gathered the pile of papers back into her file and retied the sacred pink ribbon

– which was not something Mr Branch Prosecutor was brimming with today either. Unconfident, silent, almost dour in manner. She did not greatly like Harris: a cold fish and too much of a fence-sitter in the manner of men with driving ambition. Not that one could really expect much else in view of the scandalously low rate of salaries set for CPS lawyers. It was a miracle the service ever recruited anyone of any ability.

Denis Lisle welcomed the defence counsel into his office with even more anxiety than usual. In part, this was because Mullins was everything Lisle was not: decisive and confident in style, outspoken and snappy, a veritable steamroller of a lawyer who was also, so it seemed to Lisle, less than fastidious in his professional ethics.

It was this last aspect which most worried the solicitor because, while proofing her evidence with Sharon Snow, he had run into an ethical poser. However, he didn't rush in with it, instead letting Mullins rattle on in theatrical anticipation of how he planned to demolish what he termed the Crown's *dramatis personae* – Candidate Darroch, Witch-Hunter Wilson, and Black Knight Roberts.

'Wallace willing, we shall score a triumphant no-case-to-answer at the end of me Lady Edwina's Act One.'

'Judge Wallace has heard an awful lot of Snow's bail applications.'

'Ah, but to refuse how many? None. A man immaculate in his law who hates nothing more than to be reversed on appeal. If I can rout Prosser's perjurers, Wallace may well acknowledge it and dismiss.'

'Very well,' Lisle murmured. 'But just in case it proves necessary to field our single, er, *dramatis persona*, be warned about Sharon Snow.'

Mullins grimaced in equivocation. 'Not the brightest of performers, as I recall her from Snow's previous trials, but none the less convincing for that. An element of naïve innocence about her delivery.'

'Ah, but previously called only as a character witness. This time she's material.'

'Unequivocal alibi witness,' the barrister remarked, referring briefly to her witness statement. 'Hard to foresee any hazard.'

'The difference,' Lisle persisted, 'is that, this time, she herself has doubts.'

'Ah.' Mullins's eyes narrowed. 'About his innocence, you mean? After all these years?' He resumed reading the statement only to stab at part of it in exposition. '*Here*. Due, of course, to this – the Black Knight's sly nocturnal visit, his warning for the safety of daughter Susan, his harassment and –'

'No, sir, because she's having to lie about her husband's movements. Because she knows he may very well not have been at home that morning between nine and ten.'

There was a pause, the barrister staring at the solicitor from beneath his dark, craggy eyebrows. 'She actually told you this, Lisle?'

'What she said was: *What if they ask about the doctor's?*'

'The doctor's?' Mullins of course recalled that her statement made no reference to any doctor. 'She went out to the surgery?'

'Yes.'

'Ah. And she's afraid Snow could have gone out then?'

'Naturally.'

'What time was it?'

'She's vague on that. The appointment was for nine. She was early and she thinks she was about his third patient. Third or fourth.'

Pause. 'So this –' Mullins slapped in frustration at the witness statement – 'this is unsafe.' Then, hastily preempting any answer to that one: 'What did you instruct her to do?'

159

It was, of course, the crucial question, and for just a moment Lisle was tempted to bait the grizzly bear and pretend he had urged Sharon to withdraw her evidence.

'I told her what I imagined would be your instruction, sir, given the circumstances.'

'Which was?' Then, crisp with impatience. 'Come, man, don't dangle me.'

'To stick to her original statement, make no reference to the doctor and to trust that the other side don't find out.'

'Thus, by default, to perjure herself.'

'Was I wrong?' Lisle reached for the telephone. 'I can most easily remedy that instruction.'

'*No*.' The barrister shook his head, eyes averted, wishing to God solicitors wouldn't draw him into these vexatious ethical no-go areas. 'No, well, not yet at any rate. As I said earlier, Wallace willing, we shall win an end of play with Prosser's closure. If not, well then, we shall have to see.'

Chapter Fourteen

As usual, from the start, the personality of this particular judge set the style of the trial. As a tough, no-nonsense bencher constantly alert for tricks or improprieties, Wallace ensured his total authority over the proceedings. No figurehead or dozing presence in wig and purple but a participant of the first order to whom counsel deferred at every step – particularly so the wily Mullins who, for once, forebore any challenges to the constitution of the jury. Aware, too, that Wallace fancied himself with the ladies, not least the spectacular Edwina, Mullins resorted from the outset to an uncharacteristically low profile, giving madam her head in the hope that, getting cocky with the tyrant, she would lose it.

This strategy was soon put to the test when, prior to her opening address, Edwina Prosser rose with a request for a screen.

'Your Honour, the Crown's first witness will be the ten-year-old victim, called to give evidence of the assault. Your Honour, in view of the acute distress occasioned to such child witnesses in court, the Crown request the use of a temporary screen to, as it were, shield her from the close proximity of her alleged assailant merely a couple of metres away.'

'A screen of what, Miss Prosser?'

'Of light plywood, Your Honour, placed just across this space here between the witness-box and the dock.'

The layout of the Crown Court was relatively modern, the raised witness-box close beside the dock on the judge's right, so that both defendant and witness faced across to the raised jury box on the opposite side.

Between them, in the well of the court, the defence team was seated on the left below the jury while the Crown's lawyers, police and forensic experts were massed on the right.

'Mr Mullins?'

'Your Honour, I submit my learned friend's application amounts to little more than pantomime calculated to impress the jury rather than to spare the witness.'

'Miss Prosser?'

'Perhaps my learned friend is himself more adept at theatricals than feelings. Also, Your Honour, he was not to know that, pursuant to the assault, the child has been suffering from a condition known as post-traumatic stress disorder. Patently, it is desirable to minimize her anxiety, if only in the interests of accurate testimony. Doubtless, this is why His Honour Judge Thomas Pigot last year saw fit to allow the erection of a screen at the Old Bailey in the case of R. versus – '

'Yes, Miss Prosser, I'm sure we are all aware of Judge Pigot's precedent. Mr Mullins?'

'Quite so, Your Honour,' the defence retorted, bobbing up, 'except that, in that case, the accused were all well known to the child witnesses, being in fact close relatives. In this trial, at the specific request of my learned friend, the defence has agreed that the witness be allowed to test her earlier identification by photograph by now confronting the accused in person. I submit that the *subsequent* erection of this, er, wooden barrier would serve solely to bemuse and prejudice the jury.'

The judge was noting down these pros and cons in some detail, for Mullins was right about his aversion to appeals, all the more likely in this case what with Snow's adeptness as a cellblock lawyer and his counsel's appetite for fees. Furthermore, unlike brother Pigot, he had no stomach for setting precedents.

'Application rejected, Miss Prosser. Prejudiced against the defendant we must not be.'

'Your Honour, quite so.' She bobbed in acknowledgement, resentful of Wallace's chauvinism but prepared, for reasons of strategy, to avoid a scrap so early in the proceedings. 'None the less, Your Honour, while conceding on that issue, the Crown would request that, at the very least, the presence of a social worker be permitted in the box with the child.'

'Mr Mullins?'

'Your Honour, the defence can merely echo its previous objection: such a ploy would surely serve the interests more of pantomime than of justice.'

'Hm.' Wallace finished his note, then eyed Edwina. On this one, in the interests of balance if not of justice, he was inclined to yield. 'The Crown intends to call this social worker as a witness?'

'Your Honour, no. Her name is Miss Heanley, key worker on the case and also present as an observer at the tape-recorded interview with the child. However, she is not material to the Crown's case.'

'Very well.' It helped that Wallace was aware of Miss Heanley through her reports on juveniles. 'This video-tape recording – I trust the Crown is not seeking to introduce that?'

Edwina gave him a rueful smirk as she shook her head. 'In the absence of any established precedent, Your Honour, regretfully not.' She glanced at Mullins. 'Although I understand my friend has viewed the tape with a view to possible rebuttal.'

'Mr Mullins?'

'Viewed but not pursued, Your Honour,' Mullins quipped, bobbing up. He was in fact still baffled as to why old Lisle had pressed him to view the tape, given how deeply distressing it was to sit through. Utterly suicidal to have let any jury view the thing, for all that it

163

showed the child as possibly equivocal about Snow's photograph. Odd fellow, Lisle: defended Snow all these years with unvarying success, yet capable over that tape of such grievous lack of judgement. It was almost as though he had decided that, hang it, if Mullins was to share the defence plum, he should also have to choke on the stone.

Edwina Prosser, aware of the current antipathy towards opening speeches by counsel, kept hers short and pithy. Then, before calling the child, she asked His Honour to remind those on the press benches that reporting restrictions prohibited them from publishing the name and address of the girl and her family.

Finally, she requested that, since Selina was both intelligent and aware for her ten years, she should be allowed to take the oath so as to give sworn evidence. Vigorous objections from Mullins that whereas this *might* be discretionary, the defence would most emphatically expect that any evidence given by a mere ten-year-old, however bright, should be corroborated.

Objection upheld by the appeal-wary judge after first examining various school reports and assessments of Selina. His ruling was received without surprise by Edwina, who glanced curtly at Mullins as she resumed. 'None the less, Your Honour, I trust my friend will not object to it as pantomime if we remove our, er, fancy dress so as to minimize the formality of these proceedings for the young witness.'

Mullins glanced for a lead from the judge, who paused briefly before exchanging his wig, sash and robe for a jacket. Edwina followed suit, sliding a grin at Mullins as he, too, disrobed.

All eyes on the entrance as Selina was at last led in, Janet Heanley holding her hand. She was dressed in school uniform and had her long plait pinned up Dutch-style in a coil at the back of her head. After a single panic-stricken glance around the court, she lowered her gaze to stare fixedly at the floor, allowing herself to be led along the court and up the steps into the box like a blind person.

'Miss Heanley,' the judge remarked politely, 'should you feel it necessary at any stage to address the witness, please do so audibly so there can be no suspicion of prompting on your part.'

Wallace paused for Janet's nod, then eyed the bowed head of the child. 'You may look up at me, Selina. There are certain things I wish to explain.' He waited, nodding briefly to Janet who hugged an arm around the girl, encouraging her to look up. Selina did so for barely one second, then looked down again in renewed terror. 'Selina, it is important that you speak up when answering questions because we all need to hear what you say. Also, we would very much like to see your pretty face when you answer.'

Patronizing and sexist, Edwina thought as, following a nod from Wallace, she began her examination. She had met the girl briefly outside, long enough to explain what was expected of her and to realize she would be having to coax responses from a desperately scared child. It had been for this reason Edwina hadn't pushed the issue of the oath, regarding it more as a votive plea to be sacrificed in return for other concessions . . . such as the microphone she now successfully requested for Selina to speak into.

'Your name is Selina and you live with your parents in a house beside Thicket Common? . . . Miss Heanley, would you kindly hold the microphone up for Selina?' The prosecutor also moved closer so as to make things more intimate. 'Yes, Selina?'

The magnified whisper in confirmation sounded oddly sinister.

'And were you out with your dog William on Thicket Common on the morning of the twelfth of February last?'

Well over four months' delay, the police and forensic

investigations having been completed within a week or so but the trial held up solely for lack of Crown Court facilities. Not that Selina was likely to forget the incident itself; quite the contrary, she was haunted by it. Yet the pædiatrician's efforts at treatment could be expected to make little progress until she had the distress of this trial behind her as well. None the less, Mullins would surely lay it out in a big way to the jury how four months was an eternity to a young mind, the child's memory for accurate detail eroding with every day's delay.

'Yes or no, Selina?'

'Yes.' Yet it was little more than a hiss breathed into the microphone. Oh dear. Trouble, dire trouble, unless she could find more tongue than this.

'And on that occasion, were you attacked by a stranger so that you had to be taken to hospital?' Leading her along like this was all very well for starters, but Mullins would be vigilant as a hawk when it came to details. 'Yes or no?'

'Yes.'

'Selina, would you please look around the court and tell us whether you can see the person who attacked you on that occasion?' Pause, the child seemingly frozen into inactivity. 'Look around, Selina, and if you see that person, just point.'

From where she stood beside the witness-box, Edwina could see the gentle urging of the social worker as, her arm around the child, she tried to prompt her to raise her head.

'Look around, please, Selina.' Another lengthy pause until at last the girl's head eased up sufficiently to meet the prosecutor's eyes – but registering blank terror, for heaven's sake. Edwina smiled in encouragement. 'That's the idea. Now look around.'

Subtly, holding on to the child's petrified gaze, Edwina inclined her head slightly towards the dock, attempting to signal attention in that direction, noting as she did so the social worker's subtle pressure to ease Selina around towards the man seated close beside them. Abruptly, in a series of panic-stricken peeps, Selina's eyes flickered up in apparent search, tears welling up as she did so. Round, Edwina willed her, round further.

More peeps, more tears, more pressure from Janet who had now eased back so as to minimize any possible blocking of vision in the one vital direction . . . while, alongside them, barely a couple of metres distant, Snow sat in apparent nonchalance, his jaw working, his lips curled in contempt for the laboured, faltering procedure beside him . . . until suddenly, her gasp dramatically amplified by the microphone at her mouth, the girl saw him.

Abruptly she swung away, hunching down in shock, the tears yielding into sobs as the prosecutor prompted the final confirmation. 'Point, Selina. Point to where you saw the person. Just point.'

There was a tense pause, the sobs increasing. Tentatively, Janet touched the child's arm, urging her to raise it . . . which, finally, she did, pointing aside towards the dock as she continued to huddle wretchedly against the social worker.

'Thank you, Selina.' The prosecutor glanced at Mullins before addressing the judge. 'I trust my learned friend accepts that as positive.'

'Mr Mullins?'

The defender hesitated, weighing the likely impact of the child's behaviour. The hazard lay in alienating the jury members who, although eight men to four women, mostly had the look of parents about them. Finally, to Edwina's acute relief, he bobbed up in wry acceptance. 'I would none the less point out, Your Honour, that it requires only the most basic knowledge of courtroom layout for the witness to know *where* to look and point – a child who, so my learned friend informs us, is indeed of above-average awareness.'

'Miss Prosser?'

'When it suits him, my learned friend claims Selina is too immature to take the oath, yet now he attributes a sophisticated knowledge of courtroom layout. Well, well.' She turned to find Selina had now disappeared from view, having been eased down by Janet on to the little bench in the witness-box.

'If the child could perhaps be allowed a short break?' the social worker asked.

Edwina hesitated, considering whether to cut her losses. The Crown had got its identification of the attacker confirmed, after all, and would be producing medical evidence of the result of his attack. Moreover, the more information Edwina now tried to draw from the girl – if *any*! – the more she would open her to subsequent cross-examination. Cut out now on the grounds of compassion, however, and Sam Mullins would be virtually obliged to follow suit.

'Your Honour, in view of Selina's persisting distress, the Crown is loath to prolong her ordeal further.' She bowed and sat down.

'Mr Mullins?' Judge Wallace eyed the defence team sternly, anxious to be rid of the snivelling child: untidy, unruly, embarrassing and emotional in an arena best purged of all these elements.

Mullins, getting the message, bobbed up only briefly. 'No examination, Your Honour.'

'Thank you.' The judge turned to nod to Janet. Then, as the social worker eased the sobbing child to her feet and started to lead her down from the witness-box: 'You are a very brave little girl, Selina. Thank you for coming here today. You can now go away and forget all about the ordeal.'

Hypocrite, Edwina thought as she and the others started to dress up once again in their absurd robes and wigs, trust him not to say *which* ordeal.

Chapter Fifteen

Dora Darroch's grip was tight on the edge of the box as she forced herself to look across at the defence lawyer. Such confidence as she had managed to generate prior to the trial had taken several knocks – such as when that inspector had come up in his flash suit to remind her, please, to avoid any reference to that visit to the CID office when they'd checked through her statement – such as seeing that tearful little girl led out just as she herself was summoned into court, where indeed she had found herself confronted by an ocean of dark, apparently hostile eyes. What the bloody hell, Dora girl, you're stark raving bonkers ever to have let yourself in for all this! Yet worse by far was the remorseless probing of this man's cross-examination. Somehow, merely by going over it all again and scrutinizing what she had just stated in chief to the prosecutor, he was able to insinuate if not that she was lying, at least that she was a vague, imprecise woman far from certain about the presence of the accused man at the common four months ago.

'So in essence, Mrs Darroch, you are telling the jury that you had heard the local radio reporting this violent assault on a young girl up at Thicket Common that morning and, recalling how you had been up there with your sister's dog, you searched your mind whether you had seen anything or anyone suspicious up there at the time, yes?'

'I suppose so.'

'Yes or no?' Mullins had a disconcerting technique of interrogation, wavering mesmerically backwards and forwards as he consulted papers, often murmuring the initial question over them before suddenly swinging round to confront her with the challenge. 'Let's be fully clear on it now, madam.'

'Yes.'

'Yes what? Yes, he was behaving suspiciously?'

'I already said, he saw me and he dodged away into the trees.'

'And that aroused your suspicion?'

'Only later – after hearing it on the radio – and knowing who he was.'

The defence barrister appeared to freeze in mid-sway before looking slowly up at her. 'Knowing who he was, madam?'

'Well, yes.' Her grip was tighter than ever on the rim of the box. 'Like I said, I recognized him.'

'Quite so, Mrs Darroch, but the answer you gave just then clearly implied that your recognition of him reinforced your suspicion.' Pause, Dora staring rigidly at him. 'Knowing who he was.' Pause. 'Knowing what?'

'Well – er – about him.'

'Knowing what about him? Come, madam, if you had some prior knowledge of the accused, the jury should be allowed to know of it.'

'That – er . . .'

'Out with it, please.'

'That he was notorious for this sort of thing.'

'For what sort of thing?'

'Getting after little girls, that's what. Interfering with them. Been at it for years and years, okay. Ain't a kiddie safe to go out alone. You ask anyone on our estate, they all know him.'

'We're asking you, Mrs Darroch.'

'Well, I'm telling you!' She turned to point at Snow beside her. 'This man – he's a monster, that's what. Ought to be locked up for good and the key thrown away!'

170

There was a pause, Mullins content for her to continue airing such prejudices for as long as she chose; while Dora, aware of her mistake, glared at him, defiant and at bay.

'Perhaps, in the interests of balance, so as to help the jury keep things in proportion, we should just explore the facts, Mrs Darroch.' He turned to his junior who handed him a sheet of paper. 'Did you know that this man you accuse of being a monster in fact has a distant record of *two* related offences, for the first of which, nearly eleven years ago, he received probation; for the second, eight years ago, a suspended sentence? Since then, *nothing*, hm? Perhaps your housing estate – or in any event you, madam, have a long and unforgiving memory to sustain your obvious prejudice for so many years, hm?'

'There's been no end of others!'

'Or so you may believe,' Mullins intervened sharply. 'A belief spawned, I suggest, by your prejudice but certainly not confirmed by *any* subsequent convictions, hm?'

A pause, the swaying recommencing as the defence counsel again shuffled his papers before asking quietly: 'Is it correct that you are a candidate for election to the local parish council?'

'No.'

'Ah. One moment, please.' Mullins turned round for a brief whisper with Lisle seated just behind him before resuming to Dora. 'My mistake, you *were* a candidate at the time of this alleged offence, hm?'

'Yes.'

'Quite so. Also a member of the Neighbourhood Watch Committee on this estate of yours.'

'So what?'

'Please allow me to ask the questions, Mrs Darroch.'

'I don't see what any of that's got to do with anything, that's all.'

'Well, madam, I suggest it is indicative of the type of person you are.' He paused before elaborating. 'I suggest, you see, first that you are the sort of woman to harbour an enduring personal prejudice against a man who, as a youngster years ago, twice gave way to impulsive incidents . . .'

'Repulsive, not impulsive!'

'Please allow me to finish. Secondly, that because of your political ambitions, you are keen to be identified with the law-and-order lobby on this estate of yours, making it your business to conduct a personal vendetta against this unfortunate man in the dock.'

'Is that a question or what?'

'What I'm suggesting, Mrs Darroch,' Mullins persisted, secretly welcoming her retaliation, 'is that, pursuant to this vendetta, when you heard the radio report of the assault that day, you assumed it was him and you then contrived this whole fiction of seeing Mr Snow at the scene of the crime that morning.'

'No!'

Mullins removed his bifocals to stare at her in apparent distress before resuming the ploy of checking through his papers.

'Do you recall insulting Mrs Sharon Snow one evening last October in Changit's Corner Store?'

'What? *No*.'

'No you deny it or no you do not recall it? We shall be hearing from Mrs Snow later with the details.'

'Of course she'll swear to anything to help him.'

'You deny it?'

'*Yes*.'

'None the less, after your outburst earlier – your condemnation of Mr Snow as a monster – you can hardly deny prejudice against him.'

'I'm a mother with a daughter of thirteen, and there hasn't been a day in the last eight years I haven't been worried sick in case that evil creature gets his hands on her. Yes, I'm prejudiced. But that doesn't alter the fact that I *saw* him up there at about nine-thirty that morning. I was definitely there and it was definitely him.'

'Or so you thought afterwards, hm?'

'I don't imagine things like that.'

'Well, fortunately, madam, that is for the members of the jury to decide.'

And scant prospect, Taff reflected as he scanned their twelve faces from where he sat beside Harris, of their believing her. Mullins had taken a calculated gamble, weighing the impact of Dora's demonstrable prejudice against the damage of revealing Snow's two prior convictions. Oh well, if nothing else, Dora had at least achieved that; at least, for the remainder of the trial, the twelve would be staring across at Snow's supercilious presence in the knowledge that, guilty or not of this one, he had been convicted of indecency in the past . . . proof of nothing, of course; yet an emotional bias for all that. It was doubly handy since the Crown Court was way across in the next county, distant enough from Marlbury to ensure that the name and reputation of Leonard Snow meant nothing to any of the jury members.

Edwina Prosser limited her re-examination of Dora to the purported facts of identification before releasing her from the witness-box in favour of the consultant pædiatrician, Dr Wilson.

As an expert witness, Anita Wilson had been allowed to be present in the court to see both the débâcle of Selina and the discrediting of Dora Darroch. Now follow that, she reflected ruefully as she moved across to enter the witness-box, feeling like a relay-racer handed the losing baton.

However, although nervous, she did have the benefit of past courtroom experience. Indeed, one of her most crucial steps, both towards giving effective evidence and also towards dealing with abused youngsters, had been to purge her own sense of embarrassment. To achieve this, albeit to the huge alarm of her family, she had cultivated the bizarre practice of shouting out the various crude words to do with genitalia and excrement around the house, louder and louder and louder, so as to apply the principles of aversion therapy and, through strident familiarity, to counter her own middle-class inhibitions.

'Please tell the jury, Doctor, what it was that led you to conclude the injuries to Selina were of a sexual nature.'

Anita turned to the judge to request the distribution of anatomical diagrams and also photographs of the injuries, duly waiting while they were checked by Mullins and copies then distributed to the jury. She then commenced a detailed account of the injuries – areas where the vaginal tissue had been found to be torn, others where it was bruised and so on. From this, drawing on her extensive past experience, she explained that although the penetration had been extremely violent, the absence of semen on swabs analysed at the forensic labs meant she could not confirm rape and could hence do no more than confirm digital penetration.

Edwina then asked the consultant to elaborate on the psychological injuries. Objections to this, the defence urging that the doctor should avoid speculation. Largely impossible, of course: akin to urging an Abstractionist to paint a stark representation of what is actually there.

'Certainly,' Anita began, regardless, 'there is a well-defined condition clinically known as PTSD – Post Traumatic Stress Disorder. The symptoms shown by Selina broadly conform with that: anxiety and guilt, causing such as insomnia and nightmares; also a terror of open spaces, specifically Thicket Common beside her home where she now flatly refuses to go.'

Pause to sip water before adding: 'You saw how distressed she was here in court. But even at school she's phobic about joining the other children out in the playground. In fact, given the choice, she would shut herself away at home and avoid all contact with the outside world.'

'Doctor,' the judge intervened, 'excuse me, but you referred earlier to the child's feeling guilt.'

'Typically so, yes, sir.'

'Some of the jury may misunderstand that. Are you, for instance, implying that Selina was in some degree party to the sexual act?'

'Emphatically not, Your Honour.' Anita forced herself to pause so as not to rush this aspect. 'It is a characteristic of sexually assaulted victims of all kinds that they often suffer chronic feelings of guilt, sometimes for years afterwards.'

'But, Doctor, guilt over what?'

'They see themselves as being in some way responsible for provoking the assault. The incest victims can be the worst, brainwashed by the perpetrators into seeing themselves as tarty little seducers. But equally, the rape victim will often find self-blame over, say, going out alone somewhere and laying herself open to attack.'

'But, excuse my persistence, Doctor, what about the case of Selina?'

'Much the same, Your Honour.' Again the pædiatrician paused so as not to rush it. 'In point of fact, Selina blames herself acutely because her mother had told her always to keep the dog out on the open part of the common and, if it went off into the trees, *not* to follow it. Also, although she carried an alarm device in her pocket in case of attack, when the man got hold of her and started his assault, she froze completely – another very usual victim response, I'm afraid – and was totally unable to resist him, much less sound the alarm in her pocket.' Pause. 'She feels guilty, too, for that – for freezing and failing to resist or fight back when, in point of fact, the *freeze* response appears to be a psycho-hysterical response over which the victim has no control.'

'Thank you.' Judge Wallace nodded, face lowered as he finished his note, then glanced up for her to continue.

'Well, in short, sir, Selina is a classic victim of random sexual assault. As to how long this condition could persist? Well, as Your Honour rightly observed, now at last she can start to put this, the second of her ordeals, behind her. But in many PTSD cases of this severity, mental scars may never be fully erased.'

Anita would have liked to add how deeply she felt for the plucky little girl who, until four months ago, had been so lively and free but was now so changed and injured. Instead she turned to face cross-examination by the defence.

Barrister Mullins had long since learned to resist evaluating what so-called expert medical witnesses actually said in evidence. So far as he was concerned, they were hostile witnesses who, regardless of how persuasive, it was his duty to discredit. Indeed, the more persuasive, the more vigorously the advocate would rise to the challenge. What better dining-out material with which to regale his Inner Temple colleagues than a cut-and-thrust replay of how he had humiliated and seen off his latest lady consultant! It was all solidly professional, after all, his victims having presented themselves as authorities in their field, exacting high fees for their professed expertise. So it was fair game if their pontifications took a mauling under cross-examination from a lawyer for whom the *Lancet* was as essential reading as the *Law Review*.

'Dr Wilson, would you kindly tell the court what first led you to this sensitive and highly-specialized field of child sexual abuse?'

Anita glanced involuntarily from Mullins to the prosecutor, well aware of where such personal questions could lead and unsure of her need to answer. 'Although I started in infectious diseases of children, I gradually came to realize one had an obligation to become more fully informed in this field.'

'An obligation? Could you please enlarge on that?'

'Examining numerous young children over the years, one became increasingly conscious of the high proportion who presented with indications of abuse, both physical and sexual.'

'But, madam, surely . . .'

'If I may be allowed to finish, sir. As a pædiatrician, I felt it my duty to explore those indications. However, as you just said, it is a highly specialized field, so I decided to extend the clinical experience I'd already acquired in hospital by also taking on community child health work outside – a specialist field in which I have for several years now had BMA accreditation.'

'You see, Dr Wilson, the jury may well be familiar with the way this vexed controversy was highlighted by the public inquiry into the allegedly over-zealous activities of your colleagues in Cleveland. The aura of witch-hunting which surrounded numerous of the cases undertaken by . . .'

'Your Honour,' Edwina Prosser intervened sharply, 'if it is my learned friend's intention to try and tar the witness with the Cleveland brush, it is only proper to remind the jury that Dr Wilson was called in to examine and treat this ten-year-old victim of a random assault. No question of her initiating witch-hunts, hazarding family unity or any such.'

'Mr Mullins?'

'Your Honour, my learned friend is jumping the gun,' the defence counsel responded smoothly. 'My reference to Cleveland was solely to raise with the witness the possible over-zealousness of some practitioners in this exacting and controversial branch of science.'

Judge Wallace eyed the Crown's lawyer briefly, then turned to the consultant. 'Well, Dr Wilson, how zealous were you in your examination of the victim?'

Anita turned to face the judge. For all Wallace's show of fairness, she trusted him no more than the defence counsel, both of them brothers of the legal fraternity with its deep-rooted tradition of male chauvinism. And nowhere, she felt, was that tradition more blatantly enshrined than in the way the rules of evidence and procedure in child indecency cases were so heavily slanted in favour of the defendant and against the victim: burden of proof, children lie, guilty until proved innocent, no substitute for live evidence . . . all the old clichés of the molester's charter.

'Sufficient, I trust, Your Honour, to satisfy the high standards of competence expected of any pædiatric consultant.' She turned back to face Sam Mullins. 'If you're hoping to imply that I'm an over-zealous woman prejudiced in favour of the victim, I'd like to point out that detached objectivity is a cardinal rule of examination and diagnosis.'

Counsel inclined his bewigged head in wry acknowledgement of her spirit, silently resolving to cut his losses and let her go. He should have done so there and then instead of going for the one final point.

'And the conclusion you reached, Dr Wilson, was of digital penetration only, yes? No semen, no rape, just handling the girl, hm?'

'He could, of course, have raped her, but using a sheath so as to avoid leaving traces of semen which could have been used to identify him by DNA matching. However, given the absence of semen traces, Dr Shanks and I had little alternative but to conclude digital. Which, sir, is why he was charged only with causing grievous bodily harm and indecent assault – ' she turned to stare pointedly at the sullen man in the dock – 'instead of the full rape charge, even though what the poor child suffered was every bit as vile and as damaging as rape.'

Chapter Sixteen

Edwina Prosser checked her notes and then smiled encouragingly across at the policeman in the witness-box. 'Now then, Mr Roberts, we've heard details of the forensic tests confirming that the trace of saliva on the chewing-gum was, by a probability factor in excess of ten thousand to one, saliva from the accused. Please tell the jury exactly where this piece of gum was found.'

'On the ground at Thicket Common close to where Selina had indicated to us that she was assaulted. If I may be allowed to submit photographic evidence to show the exact positions?'

So far so good, Taff thought as the usher distributed the photographs. But then, this is the easy part – unlike when Butcher Mullins gets going.

'So, together with the two women police officers, you conducted a comprehensive search in this area?'

'Yes – along with a dog-handler with a Labrador noted for scenting out evidence. However, in the event, I was the one who noticed it on the ground.'

'This was how long after the incident?'

'Three days. The day after we finally got the victim out of hospital to show us where to start searching.'

'Three days, during which time, what had been the weather pattern?'

'Fortunately for us, very still and inclined to be misty – certainly no rain or wind – otherwise I dare say it would have been obscured by blown leaves of which, as you can see from the photographs, there was no shortage.'

'You identified the gum where it lay without having to touch it?'

'I did, yes. Then, once it had been photographed *in situ*, I manœuvred it into a specimen bag for forensic analysis.'

'Why did you attach such significance to it as evidence?'

'Any such item of human detritus – a sweet-paper, a cigarette-end, whatever – would be handled in an identical fashion.'

'This was routine procedure?'

'It was, yes.'

'Did you in fact find anything else meriting analysis?'

'Some fibres of cloth, located on the bark of the oak tree visible in exhibit photograph D. On examination, these turned out to match the fibres of beige-dyed terylene from the victim's anorak.'

'Thank you.' Edwina nodded, checking her watch, then her list of examination notes, and trying to subdue her sense of unease. Things were not going well: the collapse of the child, whereas no great surprise, had been a severe loss. Mullins's demolition of Dora Darroch, however, had been a far worse blow, not only to the Crown's case but also to Edwina's confidence. DI Roberts, for all his honest, open style, *must* have known of the woman's prejudice beforehand; his precautionary revisions of her initial statement indicated that. Yet he had omitted to forewarn Edwina of it. Why? Simple over-zealousness to nail Snow? He had revealed that zealousness months earlier during the briefing on the Vicky Bates case; so how much more so now that Selina Binks had suffered this even more violent assault?

A crusader, then? Driven by zeal or resentment to make very sure this time that it stuck? Not perhaps actually to the extent of *recruiting* the Darroch woman to give false evidence, but quite probably turning a blind eye to her perjury. And if that, then what of this fortuitous piece of chewing-gum? Sam Mullins, student of police tricks and gimmickry that he was, would be just as alive

181

to that possibility as she was. He would see that her sword was, after all, made of cardboard and would stride confidently in to the kill.

She could sense from the DI's manner in the box that he knew he was vulnerable. For all his prior experience in court, there was that tell-tale tendency to rush his answers and overstate his case in the manner of a man who, through hidden guilt, expects and hence invites disbelief.

Her watch read 4.40 – late enough in the Crown court day to ensure adjournment before Mullins opened his attack. She had covered all the essential areas of the Inspector's evidence in chief. To tackle the remaining few options – such as, for instance, asking him what steps he and his team had taken to verify Dora Darroch's evidence – would be to gamble on the range of Mullins's assault. In the event, given her overall lack of confidence, Edwina decided it was a case of the less said the better, bobbed in conclusion to Wallace and sat down.

Taff Roberts muttered a Welsh oath, slowing the car behind a truck before pulling out on a straight stretch to race past. Bloody traffic: it sometimes seemed the whole south of England was submerging beneath more and more and more vehicles.

'None too bright in the witness-box today,' he remarked to Val Hobbs beside him.

'Rather you than me, Inspector. Anyway, it's tomorrow that counts.'

'Right,' Taff grunted, grimly conscious of the ordeal ahead of him.

'Excuse me, sir, but will you please slow down. I don't much fancy my chances with what's left of the Health Service.'

'Sorry.'

There was a pause, the WPC fidgeting and tense still

182

despite the fact that he slowed well down. 'You blame yourself, don't you, guv'nor,' she remarked abruptly. 'Excuse me speaking out, but Jacquie and me worry, you know. You had to do that for little Susan Snow. Had to. You're wrong if you blame yourself for what her father did to Selina Binks. Totally wrong.'

That blessed social worker's been saying more than her prayers, Taff reflected ruefully. But whether Val was right or not about blame, Selina's fate was reason enough for him to pursue the crusade and take steps to correct the balance of justice. So, damn it to hell, why his feelings of deceit and shame in the witness-box? Why the hesitancy and the stifling sense of guilt? Snow was the guilty one; no question of that. Harris was wrong to raise the spectre of its being some opportunist sex offender from outside. No one knew that better than Taff who had triggered the attack. So why, why, why all this conscience nonsense?

'You deny conducting a vendetta, Inspector, against this accused man here?' Mullins had evidently enjoyed a better night's sleep than his quarry, for he had launched into cross-examination with exceptional ferocity.

'Most strongly deny, yes, sir.'

'Were you acquainted with Detective-Inspector Hargreaves, your predecessor on the Indecency Unit?'

'No, sir, he left shortly before I joined the Thames Valley force.'

'You know why he left?'

'I believe he resigned.'

'You know why?'

Taff paused, glancing at Edwina who reluctantly took his panic cue and rose in objection.

'Your Honour, I fail to see what bearing this can have on the case.'

'Mr Mullins?'

'Your Honour, the defence contends that, for many

years now, Mr Snow has been the target of a persistent and vigorous vendetta by the local Indecency Unit, initially under the stewardship of DI Hargreaves and then, subsequent to his disgrace and resignation, under Inspector Roberts.'

'You intend to call this man Hargreaves to certify this?'

'Your Honour, the facts speak for themselves: my client was frequently pulled in for police interrogation and never once convicted. Ten interrogations in seven years, none of which was proved valid.'

Mullins paused for the judge's dour nod to proceed, then turned to resume his assault on the detective. 'I put it to you, Mr Roberts, that you knew very well about Inspector Hargreaves's vendetta and of the disgrace which led to his resignation; and, accordingly, on coming to fill his place, you embraced his vendetta and – '

'No, sir.'

'Doing so, Inspector, with added zeal, in a spirit of vengeance for your disgraced colleague.'

'Wrong, sir, definitely not.'

'Well, we shall see.' Mullins checked his papers. 'For a start, Mr Snow's arrests not only continued but with increased frequency. Also – '

'If I might answer, sir. Snow was arrested on legitimate inquiries following assaults on little girls, *all* of whom he admitted being with and – '

'*Alleged* assaults,' Mullins cut in sharply. 'None of them later confirmed under oath in a court, hm?'

'Only because – '

'Yes or no, Inspector?'

'Well, no, but – '

'Thank you.' Then, whiplike before Taff could resume: 'Then, further to your campaign of persecution, you were instrumental in removing the Snows' three-year-old daughter from the matrimonial home, yes?'

'The social services removed the child, sir, on a place-of-safety order on suspicion of – '

'Come now, Inspector, were you or were you not present as a party to the service of that order on the fifteenth of February?'

'The social worker concerned requested my presence as a precaution against trouble from Mr Snow.'

'Was there trouble?'

'In the event, no more than verbal abuse.'

'And what was the result of the medical examination of the child?'

'Fortunately, she was found to be normal, unmolested and in sound health.'

'Quite so. In short, yet another false accusation, yes? Yet another instance of the vendetta.'

'There is no such vendetta, sir, merely recurring suspicions which had to be investigated.'

'So you say, Inspector. Fortunately, it will be for the jury to decide whether those suspicions were warranted or indeed fabricated as part of a concerted campaign of persecution.'

He paused, glancing at Edwina who was showing signs of protest. In the event, she remained seated, hoping that Wallace would intervene. He didn't.

'The fact is, sir,' Taff observed in retaliation, 'that within eighteen hours of the return of Snow's little daughter, Selina was savagely assaulted on Thicket Common.'

'Indeed yes, giving you the excuse, yet again, to roar out to the Snows' house, siren blaring, and once again drag him off into police custody. No evidence whatsoever at that stage, just *suspicion*, yes?'

'It wasn't long before we had some evidence.'

'Ah yes. The prejudiced Mrs Darroch.'

'There can't be many parents in Marlbury without similar feelings about the man.'

'Hardly surprising, surely, Inspector, what with the persisting police vendetta against him?'

'No vendetta, sir.'

'No? Then just how would you classify your subsequent harassment of Mrs Snow?'

'Sir?'

'Come now, didn't you visit her home at approximately ten-thirty that evening?'

'Yes.'

'Why?'

'She'd telephoned to the station with a complaint. Someone had flung a half-brick at her front door.'

'And you went to investigate this incident?'

'Yes.'

'Was that normal procedure?'

'Normal, sir?'

'The detective-inspector in charge of indecency cases called out in the middle of the night to investigate a complaint of estate vandalism?'

Taff's hesitation was only momentary. What else but to brazen it out, damn it! 'Not entirely normal, no. However, the duty sergeant took the initiative of notifying me because he knew I had cause to speak to Mrs Snow on other matters. He suggested I might like to combine both roles.'

'At ten-thirty at night?'

'That's when she telephoned. I considered alerting a beat constable but then decided to respond myself.'

'Rank opportunism, surely?'

'An element perhaps – to save me calling on her next day.'

'Well, I suggest, Inspector, that your investigation of the vandalism was cursory in the extreme.'

'No, sir.'

'And that your prime objective was to get into the house that night and browbeat Mrs Snow into somehow incriminating her husband with the assault on Selina, hm?'

'No, sir.'

'You deny telling her of Mrs Darroch's evidence against her husband and then asking her how she and more so her little daughter could possibly continue to live with such a monster?'

'I deny that, yes.' Then, reaching into his pocket for his notebook: 'If I might be allowed to consult the contemporaneous note I recorded of the conversation.'

'Written down in the presence of Mrs Snow and then read back to her?'

'No. Written out shortly after I left her home.'

'In short, your version and not hers.'

Mullins shrugged in disdain, then abruptly switched his attack, a man in his element, using the skills which training and years of experience had honed rapier sharp; relishing, too, the metal of his adversary, much as a duellist welcomes a match to stretch his deadly skills.

'You were acquainted with Mrs Darroch *before* she volunteered these, er, allegations of seeing the accused at the Common that morning, were you not?'

'Not acquainted exactly . . .'

'Come now, surely you . . .'

'If I may be allowed to answer, sir?' Then, when Mullins stared evenly back at him: 'I had sat in the same room with her a couple of times at the inception of the Box Common Neighbourhood Watch Committee. I wouldn't say we'd actually *talked* together on these two occasions. Other than that, no, I'd never met her.'

'You deny telephoning Mrs Darroch on the day of the Selina assault *before* she was visited by WPC Crane and then volunteered these allegations of seeing Mr Snow at the scene of the crime?'

'Your Honour, please,' Edwina put in, bobbing up, 'my friend had the opportunity to put this to Mrs Darroch under cross-examination but omitted to do so. Most improper now to try and introduce it.'

'I withdraw the question,' Mullins remarked, satisfied that at least the possibility of such collusion had been planted in the minds of the jury. 'Did you, however, interview Mrs Darroch *subsequent* to her making this witness statement to WPC Crane?'

'Briefly, yes.'

'Why?'

'I was investigating a vicious sexual assault on a child. Perfectly legitimate to go over the evidence of a crucial material witness.'

'*Go over*, Inspector? You mean, rehearse her, perhaps, for examination on her evidence?'

'Merely to check over the details of what she'd said to WPC Crane.'

'And what steps did you take to verify this crucial material evidence?'

'I obtained statements from her work supervisor and also her sister to verify the times and the claim that she had walked the dog.'

'You did so in person?'

'As it happened, yes.'

'A woman police constable is entrusted with the statement from the crucial material witness but *you* interview the two subsidiary witnesses.'

'As it happened, yes.'

Mullins performed a little show for the benefit of the jury, glancing pointedly around at them as if to imply some sinister significance to this rather random point. Then he checked his notes prior to again switching his attack.

Taff, glad of the pause, signalled to the usher for a glass of water. The hours of evidence were starting to tell, his mind increasingly less sharp, his throat drying in mid-sentence so that he frequently had to clear it; similarly, his eyes tending to smart and require dabbing. Guilt, boyo, he reflected grimly; next thing, you'll start a migraine.

They're watching you, and all: twelve pairs of eyes, weighing and assessing, watching for signals of truth or falsehood, searching for hints of corruption.

'Now then, Inspector, this piece of, er, chewing-gum which you claim to have found so fortuitously at the scene of the crime.' Mullins paused, affecting to notice the tumbler of water. 'I'm so sorry, are you all right?'

'Perfectly, sir, yes.'

'Very well, this piece of gum. You must have exceedingly keen eyesight to locate it, as you claim to have done, on the forest floor, hm?'

'It's part of the job, sir, to search for clues. A skill which one develops with practice. Moreover, there's a clear-cut procedure, the area sectioned off and – '

'I dare say, Inspector. None the less, a tiny piece of used gum among the leafmould and twigs – extremely fortunate, you must agree.'

'It's often through such painstaking searches that crimes are solved.'

'Well, I put it to you, Mr Roberts, that your claim to have found this damning piece of evidence is false and – '

'No, sir.'

'And yet another instance of your vendetta so as to secure a conviction against this unfortunate man in the dock.'

'Definitely not. Moreover, there is no vendetta.'

'So you say. But you'll surely agree how easy it would have been for you to plant this evidence there in the woods?'

'I beg your pardon?'

'A clear enough question, Inspector. Assuming you had been able to acquire a piece of gum chewed by Mr Snow prior to that date, it would have been all too easy, yes?'

'Odd sort of assumption, sir.'

'Really, Mr Roberts? Well, let us just explore that assumption for a moment. You'd agree, it is Mr Snow's habit to chew gum?'

It was a trap, but little Taff could do about it. 'I have noticed him doing so once or twice.'

'Particularly so when under stress –' Mullins indicated the prisoner – 'such as now. Likewise, when under police interrogation.'

'If you say so, sir.'

'You had frequently had him under interrogation while in custody. Ample opportunity for you secretly to acquire and retain this piece of chewed gum . . .'

'No, sir.'

'In readiness for the next time you arrested him *on suspicion* of perpetrating an assault, yes?'

'No, sir.'

'Did you not contrive to accompany the accused and his family on a journey to Wiltshire following his release on bail last November?'

'Not contrived . . .'

'No? Isn't it a fact that you were the investigating officer who had initiated his prosecution?'

'I was, sir.'

'Most irregular, then, for you of all officers to escort him on that journey, hm?'

Taff swallowed, reaching for the glass of water. 'Under the circumstances there was no harm in it.'

'The circumstances? Well, I put it to you, Inspector, that your reason for totally disregarding procedure like that was so as to harass and persecute this man in the presence of his family.

'No.'

'Well, that is for the jury to decide.' Pause as counsel eyed the twelve, then faced back towards the witness-box. 'Did he chew gum during that journey?'

'He may have.'

'We shall hear from his wife later how you actually *gave* her husband gum to chew on that occasion. Yes?'

'No, sir.'

'Well, we shall see.'

'Hardly consistent with – ' Taff's throat dried so that he had to reach yet again for the glass before continuing – 'with this, er, so-called vendetta you're on about.'

'Sorry? What isn't?'

'Giving him gum.'

'Well now, I put it to you, Mr Roberts that, as well as harassing him, you went on that journey to Wiltshire with the specific intention of obtaining that evidence.'

'No, sir.'

'That is when you acquired this particular piece of gum.'

'No.'

'Which you later planted and then *found* at the scene of the crime.'

'Emphatically denied, sir.'

'You planted this gum,' Mullins persisted in remorseless summary, 'and also incited Mrs Darroch to volunteer her perjured evidence . . .'

'No, sir.'

'Both acts effected as part of your vendetta against Mr Snow . . .'

'No vendetta.'

'And your corrupt and determined intention to fabricate a case against the man who, from the outset, you had decided was guilty.'

'No, sir.'

'Or, to borrow the parlance current in the Metropolitan Police Force, to stitch him up, yes?'

'Absolutely not.'

Mullins turned with a rhetorical flourish to the jury, then moved to sit. 'No further questions, thank you.'

Chapter Seventeen

Edwina Prosser, although she re-examined Taff on the various lines raised during Mullins's attack, felt able to retrieve little credibility. Her questions were cautious and restrained. Worse, she felt betrayed by the engaging young detective. Why, for instance, had he not told her in advance of the place-of-safety order on the child Susan? Or of the late night visit to Mrs Snow? And why present such false confidence about the strength of Mrs Darroch's evidence? Indeed, truth to tell, she reckoned Mullins was right about the over-zealous idiot actually planting the gum.

'Your Honour,' she announced, having at last seen the policeman out of the witness-box, 'that concludes the case for the prosecution.'

She was hardly down before Mullins bobbed up, eager to get his plea in before the judge could adjourn for an early lunch. 'Your Honour, the defence has a submission.'

'A brief one, I trust, Mr Mullins.'

'Indeed, Your Honour, yes.' He checked his notes. 'Your Honour, I submit the Crown has singularly failed to establish that this accused man was anywhere near the scene at the time of the assault. On the contrary, I submit that what has emerged most clearly is that my client is the hapless victim of a sustained vendetta conducted against him over many years by the local police; hence it is apparent that such scant evidence as has been offered by the Crown has been fabricated in a trumped-up attempt to incriminate an innocent man. Accordingly, Your Honour, the defence now submit that the accused has no case to answer in law and that, accordingly, the jury should be instructed to acquit.'

'Thank you, Mr Mullins.' Judge Wallace's face remained a mask to his opinion as he finished his note and then signalled for Edwina to speak in rebuttal – which she did with vigour, duly reviewing the Crown's evidence and the points of law on which they relied. When she had finished, the judge thanked her politely, then collected his papers in readiness to stand. 'I shall consider the submission over lunch – until at least two o'clock.'

'Well, you mad chancer, how's the crusade going?'

'Diabolical, guv'nor.' There had been an element of masochism about Taff's telephoning Chiefie Walsh as promised to report on progress. A masochistic need to share his frustration. 'In fact, right now, old Pile-Driver's considering whether Snow has any case to answer.'

'That bad?' Walsh grunted in concern. 'Don't tell me you let Mr Samuel Mullins get the better of you.'

'The fly devil gambled on letting out Snow's previous so as to make him seem the victim of a long-running vendetta.'

'Ha. Shot down your phoney witness, your chewing-gum and you along with it, eh?' He gave a wry snort, and Taff could imagine those tufted eyebrows jutting in cynicism. 'Teach you to play clever buggers, lad. Takes a pro to pull that sort of stunt.' He guffawed, but not without a hint of sympathy. 'Okay, so you shot yourself in the foot – own-goal time. So just learn to steer clear of the tricks in future. Okay?'

''Bye, guv'nor.'

'Learn, damn it!'

'The hard way as usual.'

He hung up and pushed his way out of the phone-booth only to check in guilt at sight of Harris walking towards the court exit with Edwina Prosser. Sow the

193

wind to reap the whirlwind, he thought grimly. Neither lawyer wore an expression even remotely connected with hope. Both, he felt, avoided seeing him. And fair enough, since the last thing he wanted right now was to eat a pub lunch seasoned with their sense of betrayal.

Instead he ducked off along Lent Lane to the Fox and Grapes, confident that no lawyer would make such a cheapo choice. As it turned out, he was right about the Crown lawyers but wrong about the opposition, for he had hardly settled with a pint of draught Guinness when he saw old Denny Lisle ordering at the bar. It struck him as odd, less that Lisle should descend to the Fox's rowdy spit-and-sawdust so much as that he wasn't lunching with Sam Mullins.

For all Taff's cynicism over lawyers, he had some sympathy for Lisle. Moreover, since the legal aid system meant that *someone* was going to represent Snow, better old Denny than some Law Centre lefty.

In point of fact, Denis Lisle's heart was pounding like a train as he ordered a double Scotch, his eyes hunting feverishly around the crowded bar, into every corner except the one where the policeman had settled. For, although he had deliberately followed Roberts from the court, he was now suffering acute misgivings about doing so.

It was the *change* that disturbed him, the breaching of the code by which he had lived successfully enough for close on forty years. To change the rules at his age was not easy, causing his heart-rate to soar and bringing sweat to the mottled skin of his brow.

Yet change he must. Harris's example was testimony to that. For if the branch prosecutor, rising star of the CPS and son of a judge, could bend the rules so as to try and tilt the scales of justice, then so too could old Denny, hang it. Call it duty to life for once rather than to professional ethics.

'You all right, Mr Lisle? Looking a bit flushed.'

'Distinctly nervous,' the solicitor confided, easing carefully down into the space the Inspector made for him in the window nook.

'I take it your guv'nor's lunching with His Honour.'

Lisle's guffaw at the joke was rather over-loud. 'Matter of fact, I told Mr Mullins I had to go and see a young client.' He was still watchful of the faces around them. 'Best keep this as short as possible, Roberts.' He took a gulp of Scotch prior to plunging in. 'Thing is, I reckon if you and Harris can do it – to try, you know, to stop the man – well, why not me?' Then, quickly to head off Taff's response: 'Now, now, don't imagine I'm here to fish. In fact, best if you just sit there and say nothing. Thing is, you see, I've never been sure before. Well, of course, I'm not *sure* this time. Shunt myself off the case if I was. But the fact is, you see, there's a bit of, er, defence evidence, which needs testing.'

He gulped the remains of his Scotch, restless and tense, yet committed now on his desperate course. 'To do with his wife, of course. Well, naturally, being as she's our only witness. Snow would never risk exposing himself to cross-examination.' He guffawed absurdly. 'Unlike exposing himself to all those little girls. Anyway – anyway, you tell Lady Edwina – total confidence this, understood: don't tell her from me.' He waited for Taff's startled nod. 'You tell her to *ask about the doctor*.'

'What about him?'

'Just – ' Lisle was already up and on his way – 'just tell her to ask, that's all.'

'She'll want to know . . .' Taff left it in the air, for the solicitor was already away, scurrying off like a boy who has thrown a stone at the mayor in procession – or worse, Taff thought, at the Lord Chancellor.

* * *

Lady Edwina did want to know – most insistently. Not that she was refusing to ask about the doctor. But she was a great one for the tried old principle of never asking a witness a question unless you already knew the answer.

'Find out, please, Inspector. Trace her doctor and see if she had an appointment.' She gestured in rueful irony. 'Not that it'll matter one way or t'other if old Pile-Driver rules they've no case to answer.'

Judge Wallace had in fact passed a dour luncheon. He wanted nothing more than to see the arrogant little groper brought to justice once and for all; and he was seething over the bumbling ineptitude of that twit Harris and, worse, his Welsh cohort, Roberts. God's blood, if they'd decided to stitch up a case against the little rat, why couldn't they do so *properly* instead of everything coming so embarrassingly unstuck the moment Butcher Mullins got his knife out!

Yet he was surprised at Harris: he'd never have thought Mr Fifty-One Per cent would find the guts to have a go like this. Damn sure his pompous old ass of a father would never do so; credit the son with a touch more spirit in future, for all that he and Roberts had botched it so amateurishly . . . Certainly have expected a more convincing show from an ex-Met DI, too; if nothing else at the Yard, they learnt how to stitch up cases better than this . . .

'Court rise!'

The judge strode in, bowed left and right, then sat in the huge leather chair beneath the coat of arms.

'Mr Mullins, I have considered your submission. I find there *is* a case to answer. Please proceed.'

'Your Honour, yes.' Mullins bobbed, not in the least surprised, it not being an issue which carried the right of appeal. 'Members of the jury, Mr Snow's case is straightforward and simple in the extreme. The defence will show that Mrs Darroch's identification was mistaken since the accused was nowhere near Thicket Common that morning, being on the contrary at home with his wife and child. As for the chewing-gum allegedly found at the scene of the crime, the defence will show that indeed Mr Snow has for years been the target of persecution by the police to the extent of their now fabricating incriminating evidence against him.

'You will hear comprehensive evidence confirming both these aspects from the accused's wife, Mrs Sharon Snow, in a case of such essential simplicity that it would be superfluous and burdensome for you to hear it merely repeated by the accused.'

With which bland piece of verbal footwork, he signalled for the usher to call Mrs Snow.

If Sharon had been briefed on what to wear and how to behave it was badly done, for the funereal black costume and also the manner of haughty solemnity somehow both conspired to parody the snubby nose and short upper lip of her baby face. Of course she was nervous – a factor which Sam Mullins somewhat over-stressed, urging her to take her time, not to rush her answers and to do her best to speak up, please, since the jury members needed to be fully clear over what she had to say.

He took her first through the background to their marriage – the grim years of Leonard's recurring arrests which clearly had never proved other than false challenges of a man whose sole fault – if fault it was – lay in his enduring fondness for children . . . that totally innocent fondness typical of a parent drawn to the equally innocent company of young children . . . yet vindictively distorted by the police ever since his first spot of trouble as a teenager . . . years of suffering for them both, since she had been vilified by neighbours and shopkeepers, abused and spat upon in public – and, yes, once insulted by that Darroch woman there at the back of the court, whose oafish husband she was also sure had flung the brick at her door that night of Leonard's last arrest.

And, yes, it had been that pushy Inspector Roberts who had come in answer to her complaint – the same copper who had been hounding Leonard for years and who had come two nights earlier to snatch their little Susan away on that trumped-up order. He'd come pushing his way into her kitchen that second night, trying to put words into her mouth and get familiar and then, when she had told him to leave, telling her all that filth about Leonard being a threat to their precious little girl!

Passionate and tearful testimony, coaxed emotively from her by the skilled Mullins who, seemingly almost as a formality at the end, finally referred to her husband's alibi.

'You told the police at the time of his arrest at ten-fifteen that morning that he'd not been out since the previous day, yes?'

'Yes.'

'And you reaffirm that now under oath?'

'Yes.'

'He was at home with you all that time?'

Her hesitation was only brief, her head turning impulsively to the man in the dock before again staring back at the jury. 'Yes.'

'Thank you, Mrs Snow. Please remain there in case my learned friend has anything to ask you.'

'Just a few questions,' Edwina murmured, smiling at her as she stood up. 'All these years of what, not unreasonably, you interpreted as persecution – the police accusing him of sexually molesting children and your husband insisting the accusations were false – did you never wonder about him? Ask yourself if the accusations might possibly be true?'

'No.' She bit her lip, realizing the absurdity of it. 'Well, yes, but . . .'

'But what? You dismissed the doubts?'

Pause before Sharon nodded, still biting her lip.

'You would, after all, have been better placed than anyone else to know, hm?'

'Eh?'

'To know if he was up to anything like that. If he was slipping off every now and then to have his fun with any little girl unfortunate enough to encounter his prowlings, yes?'

'Your Honour – ' Mullins had his hands spread in protest at such a liberty.

Edwina bobbed in acknowledgement, inclining her head as she modified it. 'To know if he was up to what the police were *saying* he was up to, yes?'

'Yeah.' She nodded. 'I'd have known.'

'So, in weighing your evidence on that, the jury has to decide whether you assessed his version correctly *or* whether you are excessively gullible *or* whether you are excessively loyal, to the extent of lying so as to protect him from the law, yes?'

'They set him up,' Sharon remarked abruptly.

'I beg your pardon, Mrs Snow?'

'Framed him.'

'Oh? You see, the court heard earlier how your husband never denied being with all these little girls over the years – merely denied doing what they always *said* he did to them.'

'It was the police – that man Roberts – he told them kids what to say.'

'Oh? Now let's get this clear, Mrs Snow, you believed that Detective-Inspector Roberts prompted the victims into *pretending* they had been assaulted?' Edwina shot an ironic glance at the jury. 'Come now, Mrs Snow.'

'It's true! All them disgusting dolls they use with the kids. He'd use them dolls to get 'em all confused and that

'– lead 'em on so they'd make up all them filthy tales about – about Len.'

'Well, as a matter of fact, Mrs Snow – just to set the record straight for the jury – Detective-Inspector Roberts never conducts any of the interviews where these dolls are used. That part of the investigation is always conducted by a policewoman and a female social worker, both with specialized training. So you see, if that's what your husband told you, it's false.'

She paused, waiting until Sharon at last met her gaze. 'And you are still telling the jury that at no time during all your years with Mr Snow have you ever had cause to wonder –'

'No.'

'Nothing he's said or done to make you suspicious?'

'No.'

'No little clues or, say, pornographic pictures of young children in his possession?'

Sharon had her mouth open in denial only to check, recalling the photographs found after the Vicky Bates incident.

'Yes, Mrs Snow?'

'Well, like, only . . .' Her glance went involuntarily back to her husband, who gave a slight shake of his head. 'Er, no.'

'Mrs Snow, the jury is unlikely to attach any credibility to such answers if you so clearly take your cue on them from your husband. No pornographic photographs of young children?'

'No.'

'Perhaps you are forgetting the set of a dozen such pictures found hidden in his workshop when . . .' Edwina paused as Mullins rose in objection.

'Your Honour, may we know if the Crown intend to introduce any such alleged pictures in evidence?'

'They were returned to the accused after the case

against him was withdrawn some six months ago, Your Honour.'

'Then it is wholly improper for you to refer to them, Miss Prosser,' the judge rebuked her before turning to the jury. 'You will please disregard the Crown's reference to pornographic photographs of young children.'

Wallace nodded for Edwina to resume. However, instead, she started to act out a small drama pre-arranged with Harris and Roberts, the Inspector having come into court to whisper a seemingly urgent message to Harris, who passed a hurried note forward to Edwina – who, glancing at the note, now requested the court's indulgence for a moment, duly plunging into whispered conference with her team. Finally, with the flourish of a jousting knight suddenly re-armed with a fresh lance, she turned to resume to Sharon.

'Mrs Snow, a few minutes ago, I pointed out to you how the jury would eventually have to decide whether you are being loyal to this man in the dock to the extent of deliberately lying so as to conceal his guilt, yes?'

'Yes, what?'

'You remember that?'

'Yes.'

'And you maintain you have not lied to the court as yet?'

'No.'

'In answer to Mr Mullins, you said that your husband was at home with you at the time of the sexual assault on little Selina Binks – specifically between nine and ten a.m. on the morning of the fifteenth of February. Yes or no?'

Again the hesitation, Sharon inhibited less by guilt this time so much as sudden fear. 'Yes.'

'You were there at home with him at that time?' Pause. 'Yes or no, madam. Tell the jury, please.' Pause, the baby

201

face puckering now in conflict. 'Mrs Snow, what about the doctor's?'

The sob which tore from the young wife was, in truth, closer to relief than anguish.

'Well, Mrs Snow?'

'He – Leonard said not to tell about that.' She kept her face firmly away from him now. For once the man's jaw was motionless, locked rigid as she continued. 'Said how I was his only hope to prove how they was framing him again and, like, not to tell about that – about the doctor.'

Pause, the court shocked still and silent, all eyes turning now to the man who, cornered and at bay, glared back in defiance.

'So, Mrs Snow, out of blind loyalty, you agreed to lie so as to shield him?'

'He – ' the wife had to pause again as her throat tightened up – 'he gets, like, claustrophobic. Feels shut in and has to get out. That night after they brought our Susy back home from the hospital, it hit him real bad. Tension, like. Couple of hours and he was off into the night. Well, he had to, see, so as to let off steam – get out in the air, run in the open.'

She paused to fumble for a tissue and then blew her nose before resuming. 'He was back when I got home from the doctor's with Susy. Back home and taking a bath.' Pause, the woman unable now to look up.

'He was in the bath,' Edwina coaxed, 'and calling out for you to wash his clothes?'

'Eh?'

'You had his clothes in the washing machine when the police arrived.'

'Yeah – well – out all night, running and that, he was bound to be all messed up, eh.' She trailed off to a silence somehow even more damning than the words. Edwina let it run, affecting to wait while the woman snuffled into her tissue, eyes lowered, her shoulders heaving now with partial sobs.

'He's promised me,' she blurted in sudden irrelevance, 'promised, after all this we'll get right away. A total change. The Falklands or – or somewhere.'

There was another long silence, this time broken by the judge. 'You have any further questions, Miss Prosser?'

'Thank you, no, Your Honour.'

Nor had Mullins. He knew when to let well alone – knew, too, when he was beaten – knew, moreover, that he had been betrayed, by whom and when, God damn it!

He rallied as best he could for the closing address. But it was a hollow performance bordering on embarrassment. The jury went out for barely half an hour, duly returning with verdicts of guilty on both counts.

'Leonard Arthur Snow, in requesting that an additional twenty-three indecent assaults on young children be taken into account for your sentence, you have revealed the enormity of the reign of lustful terror you imposed upon the children of Marlbury. That it took so many years and so many victims before your vile ways were finally brought to light, reflects not upon the competence of the police but on the dilemmas inherent in the legal system regarding the prosecution of child sex offenders. Indeed, the officers involved in this prosecution are to be commended for their diligence and tenacity.

'Leonard Snow, it is the sentence of this court that you go to prison for ten years. Take him down.'

Chapter Eighteen

'We've collared that flasher at last, Mr Harris.'

'The nurses' home character?'

'That's right. Matron decided enough was enough: couldn't have her girls lining up at the windows for a show night after night.'

'Matron?'

'She marched out into the park, grabbed the bloke and, would you believe, clobbered him with his own torch.'

'Clobbered him where?'

'Good question. Anyway, it turned out to be one of the hospital porters.' Taff grinned, sliding the case file across. 'I'm happy to say, this'll be my last Indecency offering for you.'

'Really?' The branch crown prosecutor was not sorry: the burden of their shared secret was too heavy for him ever again to feel comfortable with the Inspector. 'Promotion?'

'Up the ladder, yes.' Taff avoided the lawyer's eyes. It had not been through ambition that he had conspired to Snow's conviction, and it was embarrassing now to reap this consequence. 'Oddly enough, I'm off back to the Yard. Not to rejoin the Met. Just on attachment for a special investigation.'

Harris grunted, struck by the irony, since such attachments were invariably for internal investigations of police corruption. Yet why not? Roberts was a crusader. For all the impropriety of his combat methods, he was on the side of the angels. Moreover, from Harris's point of view it was comforting news, since to investigate internal corruption would put Roberts's personal integrity very much on the line; so that their shared secret was locked all the more securely away between them.

'One thing, old man, before the Yard swallows you up.' Harris tried to phrase it as casually as possible, yet the lingering anxiety was there plain to hear. 'Just how did you get on to that business of Sharon Snow's appointment at the doctor's.'

'An informant, sir,' Taff rapped out, suddenly anxious to be off. 'Confidential.'

'I've racked my brains, you see, and there's only the one possible informer I can think of.'

'Well then, sir, the less said the better.' Clearly Harris wanted to know not out of curiosity but to set his careful lawyer's mind at rest.

'A matter of ethics, Inspector?'

'Suffice it to say that he was moved to confide the information because, after hearing the Crown's case, he was convinced the bulk of it was a put-up job. Fudged, as you put it. That deeply impressed him. *If Jeremy Harris can bend the rules to try and bring the man to justice*, he told me, *then so can I.*' Taff gave a curt nod, moving to open the door. 'Nice little irony, really.'